FULL PACKAGE

BY LAUREN BLAKELY

Also By Lauren Blakely

The Caught Up in Love Series (Each book in this series follows a different couple so each book can be read separately, or enjoyed as a series since characters crossover)

Caught Up In Us
Pretending He's Mine
Trophy Husband
Stars in Their Eyes

Standalone Novels
BIG ROCK
Mister O
Well Hung
The Sexy One
Full Package
The Hot One (March 2017
Joy Stick (May 2017)
Far Too Tempting
21 Stolen Kisses
Playing With Her Heart (A standalone SEDUCTIVE NIGHTS spin-off novel about Jill and Davis)

The No Regrets Series
The Thrill of It
The Start of Us
Every Second With You

The Seductive Nights Series
First Night (Julia and Clay, prequel novella)
Night After Night (Julia and Clay, book one)
After This Night (Julia and Clay, book two)
One More Night (Julia and Clay, book three)
A Wildly Seductive Night (Julia and Clay novella, book 3.5)
Nights With Him (A standalone novel about Michelle and Jack)
Forbidden Nights (A standalone novel about Nate and Casey)

The Sinful Nights Series
Sweet Sinful Nights
Sinful Desire
Sinful Longing
Sinful Love

The Fighting Fire Series
Burn For Me (Smith and Jamie)
Melt for Him (Megan and Becker)
Consumed By You (Travis and Cara)

The Jewel Series
A two-book sexy contemporary romance series
The Sapphire Affair
The Sapphire Heist

ABOUT

I've been told I have quite a gift.

Hey, I don't just mean in my pants. I've got a big brain too, and a huge heart of gold. And I like to use all my gifts to the fullest, the package included. Life is smooth sailing....

Until I find myself stuck between a rock and a sexy room-mate, which makes for one very hard...place.

Because scoring an apartment in this city is harder than finding true love. So even if I have to shack up with my buddy's smoking hot and incredibly amazing little sister, a man's got to do what a man's got to do.

I can resist Josie. I'm disciplined, I'm focused, and I keep my hands to myself, even in the mere six hundred square feet we share. Until the one night she insists on sliding under the covers with me. It'll help her sleep after what happened that day, she says.

Spoiler—neither one of us sleeps.

Did I mention she's also one of my best friends? That she's brilliant, beautiful and a total firecracker? Guess that makes her the full package too.

What's a man stuck in a hard place to do?

This book is dedicated to Dr. Khashi.
Thank you for the laser attention, and all your time!

PROLOGUE

Let's say, for the sake of argument, that you're considering living with a woman you want to screw.

After all, finding an apartment is harder than landing true love, so even if you have to shack up with the fox you've maybe, possibly, always thought was ridiculously hot, you'd do it, right?

Look, I know what you're thinking.

This can only lead to trouble. Don't sign that lease. Walk the other way.

But she's just a friend, I swear. And, hey, this is New York City. Rent is crazy expensive. Always better to share it, right? C'mon. You'd split the utilities even if it meant you were signing up to become the designated dude sounding board for all her online dating escapades.

Please. I can do that with my eyes shut. Advising her on the plenty o' fish where she's fishing is simple. I just point to the profile pic and say: he's a douche, he's a tool, he's a dick . . .

Because none of those fuckers are worthy of her.

You'd sign that lease even if you had to endure the sweet torture of seeing that beauty walk down the hallway every morning, fresh out of the shower, a tiny towel cinched around her tits.

Easy as pie.

Even if she called out, "Hey, Chase, can you bring me my body lotion?"

Ha. That's child's play.

Okay, maybe I whimpered a bit when she made the request. And I'll concede the situation was a bit hard—like, steel levels—when the towel slipped and I caught a glimpse of her perfect flesh before she yanked it up.

But still, I can handle all that, no problemo.

Want to know why?

I've done it for years, and it's my secret talent.

You see, everyone has a unique ability. Perhaps you can lick your elbow, stick your whole fist in your mouth (don't try that at home, kids), or make your eyes move in opposite directions. Impressive party tricks, to be sure.

Want to know mine? My one-of-a-kind skill will save me from a living situation guaranteed to induce an early riser in the pants that lasts round-the-clock.

Here's my special gift: I'm the king of compartmentalization, and I come equipped with separate drawers for everything. Desires and actions. Lust and feelings. Love and sex. One goes here. The other goes there. And never the two shall meet.

That's why when one of my best friends came to me with a solution that would solve a big problem for both of us, I just didn't see how anything could go off the rails.

All I've got to do is keep my hands off her, my dirty thoughts locked up, and my eyes looking the other way the next time she gets undressed.

Mere fucking feet away from me.

I can do this. I can absolutely do this.

When you're the virtuoso of resistance, nothing can knock you off your game.

Not even cohabitating inside six hundred square feet with a woman you've wanted for years.

Until the night I woke up to find her curled up next to me under the covers . . .

Chapter One

I have a theory that it takes the human brain at least three tries to fully process something when it's the opposite of what you want to hear.

Take now.

I'm on the third attempt.

Even though I can clearly hear the words the woman on the phone says, I'm sure if I repeat them in the form of a question, she'll eventually say what I want her to say. "I lost the apartment?" I try again, because soon the bad news she's serving up will magically morph into something good. Like if a rice cake turned into pizza. Preferably a cheese pie with mushrooms.

Because there is no fucking way the leasing agent is telling me *this*.

"The landlord had a change of heart," she says once more, and the sweet one-bedroom in Chelsea slips through my fingers.

I grit my teeth and suck in a breath as I pace outside the emergency room entrance at the hospital. The sidewalk is clogged with other doctors, too, as well as nurses and paramedics, not to mention visitors. I move away from them, walking along the brick exterior during this short break in my day. "But this is the fifth time a place has fallen through," I say, doing my best to keep my tone even. I don't have a temper. I don't get angry. But if I were to, this might be the reason. Because Dante was wrong. Finding an apartment in New York City is the tenth circle of hell. It's the eleventh, twelfth, and thirteenth, too.

Consider my luck so far in this impossible quest: the first apartment went bust when the landlord changed her mind. The second time, the place was rented to someone in the family. The third pad had termites. You get my drift.

"It's a tough market right now," Erica, the leasing agent, says. I gotta give her credit. She's been trying to find me four walls and a floor for more than a month. "I'll look again to see if there are any new available options."

"Thanks. My sublease is up so I'm going to be homeless soon." I turn around and pace back toward the entrance. Buying a place isn't an option. I've still got medical school debt, and doctors don't make bank the way they used to. Especially not first-year ER docs.

She laughs. "I doubt you'll be homeless. Besides, I've told you, the couch at my place has your name on it. Come to think of it, so does the bed, if you know what I mean."

I blink. I do know what she means. I just wasn't expecting to be propositioned by my leasing agent at two in the afternoon on a Wednesday.

Or a Thursday. Or a Friday. Basically, on any day.

"Thanks for the offer." I rein in my surprise because I thought she was married. And not just the regular kind of married, but the happily kind.

"You let me know, Chase. I make a great ceviche, I'm incredibly neat, and I wouldn't even charge you a dime. We could work out some other form of payment," she says with a purr.

And my leasing agent has now officially requested that I be her boy toy. Fuck. Time to grow a beard. I know I look young for my job, but young enough to be asked to be a sugar boy? I turn to the glass window of the hospital and consider my face. Clean-shaven, hazel eyes, light brown hair, chiseled jaw . . . Damn, I'm quite a specimen. No wonder she propositioned me. Maybe I should take her more seriously.

Even though I have zero interest in serving as anyone's sex slave, her offer is borderline tempting because I'm at the end of the line. I've scoured Craigslist and everyplace else, but I might as well give a kidney for a one-bedroom—that'd be easier than finding a pad in this city.

You know all those TV shows where the perky twenty-something advertising assistant nabs a swell apartment with a flower planter, bright purple walls, and a reading nook on the Upper West Side? Or when the wet-behind-the-ears dude with an entry-level post at a magazine lands a swank bachelor pad in Tribeca?

They lie.

At this point, I'd give my spleen just for a closet under a staircase. Wait, I take that back. I like my spleen. It'd have to be a closet on the first floor for me to give up an organ, even one I can technically live without.

"What do you think? You up for it?" Erica asks, in what no doubt is her best sexy-as-sin voice. "Bob said he's fine with you being here, too."

I frown. "Bob?" Immediately, I want to take back the question because I've got a sinking feeling Bob could be her vibrator, and I walked right into that one.

"Bob, my husband," she says matter-of-factly, and now I wish we were talking about a toy.

"That's quite generous of him," I deadpan. "And please let him know that while I appreciate his magnanimity, a mattress in the locker room just opened up."

I turn off my phone and head inside, my quick break over. Sandy, the curly-haired charge nurse, marches up to me, a serious look on her face as she tips her head toward the nearby exam room. But the tiniest twinkle in her gray eyes tells me my newest patient's situation isn't dire.

"Room two. Foreign body stuck in the forehead," she tells me. That's my cue to forget about square footage and unconventional living arrangements.

When I stride into the exam room, I find an angular, blond Aquaman perched on the edge of the hospital bed.

"I'm Dr. Summers. Nice threads." I flash a quick smile. Always helps to defuse the situation. And besides, if I reacted to the three-inch shard of glass sticking out of the forehead of the guy in the green costume, they should take my goddamn license away.

He shoots me a rueful grin as he glances at his getup. The polyester outfit is torn down the right arm and ripped along the thigh.

"Looks like a fun morning," I say, eyeing the crystal fragment in his skin. "Let me guess. Your forehead got intimately acquainted with a chandelier?"

He nods guiltily, the look in his eyes telling me he wasn't trying to fly.

"And let me hazard another guess." I stroke my chin. "You were trying to spice up your sex life by testing the whole idea of hanging from the chandeliers."

He swallows, gives another small nod, then an unsteady *yup*. "Can you get it out?"

"That's what she said," I say, and he chuckles. I pat his shoulder. "Couldn't resist, but the answer is yes, and there will only be a small scar. I'm excellent at stitches."

He takes a deep breath, and I get to work, numbing his forehead before I remove the glass. We chat as I go, making small talk about his fondness for superheroes, then I tell him the latest of my apartment hunt woes.

"Manhattan is crazy," he says. "Even in commercial real estate, it's all gone through the roof." Then he adds, almost sheepishly, "Though, I can't complain since that's my business."

"Smart man. Square footage in this city is like a precious jewel," I say as I finish work on the stitches.

Twenty minutes later, I've sewn up his forehead, and a nurse returns with the shard in a plastic Biohazard bag. She hands it to me, and I pass it on to the rightful owner.

"A souvenir of today's visit to the ER," I tell the guy, and he takes the bag.

"Thanks, Doc. The sad thing is we didn't even get to the main event."

"That's why it's an urban myth. You can't really do it while hanging from the chandelier. And hey, next time you're feeling adventurous, take a cooking class and then go home and use the table for dessert, okay? But make sure it's a nice, smooth wood because I don't want to have to remove a three-inch splinter from your gluteus maximus. That's not as good a war story."

He nods crisply. "I promise. No more acrobatics."

"But kudos on having a woman who likes you that much," I say as we leave the room.

He tilts his head. "How'd you know she likes me?"

I nod toward the row of chairs in the waiting room at the end of the hallway. A dark-haired woman in a busty emerald-green costume nibbles on her lip and checks her watch. When she raises her face, her eyes light up as they land on Aquaman.

"I'm guessing the mermaid brought you in? And waited for you?"

"Yeah," Aquaman says with a dopey smile as he looks at his woman.

"Bed tonight. Use the bed, man," I say in a low voice.

He gives me a thumbs-up as he leaves.

And, that's today's latest chapter in the tales of the naughty deeds that land you in the ER. Yesterday, it was a zipper malfunction. Last week, it was a fracture from a back handspring. Yeah, you don't want to know what was fractured.

* * *

Later, when my shift ends, I change into my street clothes in the locker room, button my jeans, and tug on a T-shirt. I rake my fingers through my hair, grab my shades, and leave the workday behind me. The second the doors slide shut at Mercy Hospital, I turn off the medical portion of my brain, plug in my headphones, and crank up the audiobook I've been listening to lately. It's on the theory of chaos, and it keeps me company as I head to Greenwich Village to meet a friend.

Once downtown, I leave the subway in a throng of New Yorkers on a warm June day and make my way to the Sugar Love Sweet Shop to meet my friend Josie.

Yes, this friend happens to possess boobs.

Because I have another theory—men and women can be friends. Great friends. Even if the woman happens to be the owner of the most fantastic pair of breasts this man has ever seen. A body is a body is a body. I can appreciate her figure empirically, in all its curves and softness, and that doesn't mean I want to hang from the chandeliers with her, or even screw her on a table.

Fine, I'll concede she's totally table screwable, but I don't let myself think of Josie that way.

Even if she looks amazing in that pink scoop-neck T-shirt and a cute little polka-dot apron tied around her waist.

When she spots me, she waves and calls me into the candy shop.

I go, and my mouth is only watering because I like sweet things.

CHAPTER TWO

Josie dangles a red fish in front of me.

"Caught it today," she says with a boastful nod at the tiny treat in her hand. "Fresh from the candy shop shelves."

"Did it put up a fight?"

She shakes her head as she drops the fish in its plastic bag. "Nope. It succumbed to my credit card. Reeled it in, just like that." She snaps her fingers.

We're at Abingdon Square Park, a small triangular patch of green at the edge of the Village. It's one of the few parks that feels like its own island in Manhattan, and we settle onto a navy blue wooden bench. We're not far from the sweet shop where she finished her sushi candy-making class.

She takes a new treat from her bag, and holds it in her palm. "You ready?"

I open my mouth. "Pop it in, baby."

Yeah, maybe that sounded dirty.

Who cares? I don't, nor does Josie, who also happens to be the little sister of my best bud, Wyatt. She's requested I serve as her guinea pig tonight. The first taste test? A Swedish Fish roll, as she calls it. The red gummy is parked atop a Rice Krispies Treat center and wrapped in a green Fruit Roll-Up.

Moments like this remind me that perspective is key. Because, man, my life could be worse. Sure, I'm going to be living the Airbnb lifestyle any day now, bouncing from lumpy couch to lumpier futon, but sweetness is about to land on my tongue.

I bite into the candy roll, and it's a carnival of deliciousness. My eyebrows wriggle, and I nod approvingly as I finish chewing. I adopt an over-the-top restaurant critic's voice. "Just the perfect mix of marshmallow goodness that pairs ever so wonderfully with the tang of the Fruit Roll-Up. Add in the flavor sensation of the perennial favorite, Swedish Fish, and you have a masterpiece on your hands."

Josie's a baker, but not just any baker. She's a world-class *dessertier*. I don't know if that's a word, but it fucking should be given how this woman can wield a mixer and a baking pan. There's nothing sweet that she can't make taste like a party in your mouth. Probably why her taking over her parents' old shop, Sunshine Bakery, has been such a success.

Her eyes widen at my masterpiece compliment. "Really? You're not just saying that, are you?"

I'm stone-faced as I answer her. "I never lie about treats. Case in point. Remember the time you made those chocolate chip cookies that contained the world's worst food item?"

"You still can't say the name of it, can you?"

I close my eyes, an involuntary shudder running down my spine. "Just trying to block out the memory of . . ." Taking a deep breath, I force out the next word. "Raisins." When I open my eyes, I'm sure they're still laced with horror as I recall what she did to those helpless cookies. "Seriously. How could you defile something as wonderful as a chocolate chip cookie with a . . . dried grape?"

She shrugs helplessly. "That's how you discover what works and what doesn't work in the kitchen. You have to try. I was trying something new. Cowboy cookies with chocolate chips, coconut and—"

I clasp my palm over her lips. "Don't say it again." I release my hold on her mouth, and she rolls her eyes then mouths *raisins.*

I cringe. "Anyway, these sushi rolls are the opposite. They're perfect. But why'd you need to take a class? Why not just follow a recipe?"

Her answer is simple. "I like taking classes, and I want these desserts to be the best. Plus, the woman who runs that sweet shop has the best candies. Those aren't regular Swedish Fish that you can buy in a grocery store. They're hand-made from her family recipe. That's why I wanted you to meet me as soon as class ended. To taste them fresh."

"Are you going to serve them fresh?"

She nods excitedly and spreads her hands wide, the silver, heart-shaped ring on her index finger glinting in the evening sun. "Here's my plan. I thought I'd start offering a new fun and quirky treat each day. Like candy sushi on Mondays at three, and then on Tuesdays I'd do coconut chocolate chip cookies, minus the food item that shall not be named."

I mouth *thank you.*

"On Wednesday afternoons I'd offer a grapefruit macaron, for instance. And I can market the shop more on social media like the food trucks do. It'll be like appointment treats daily at the Sunshine Bakery."

"That's brilliant." I clear my throat, sigh deeply, and set a hand on her arm. "But I need to break this to you. No one likes grapefruit. Not even in a macaron."

Her green eyes shine like she has a secret. "Ah, but you've never tried my grapefruit macaron. I'll make that for you next. It's delish. I promise," she says, then reaches up to tighten her ponytail. Her dark brown hair is streaked with pink near the tips. Normally shades of bright colors in the locks do nothing for me, but on Josie, it just works. It suits her personality. She's bright and outgoing. Friendly and happy. She's exactly the type of person who can rock pink-streaked hair *and* selling cake, cookies, and seven-layer bars at a cheery bakery on the Upper West Side, plus sushi candy, too.

She has the whole look—the soft curves, the inviting smile, the warm eyes, the fun hair, and the upbeat attitude. Like it's a surprise this woman became one of my closest friends after I met her about ten years ago. It's impossible *not* to like Josie.

And I'm not even talking about her rack. See? I'm so well-behaved.

She gives me two more treats to try, and neither one floats my boat. I tell her that each time, and she simply nods and says thanks. Dipping her hand in the bag, she grabs what looks like a Twinkie sushi roll wrapped in taffy to represent the seaweed.

"Try this one," she says, handing me a slice as a summer breeze rustles the branches of a nearby tree.

I arch an eyebrow in question. "Aren't Twinkies bad for you?"

She winks at me. "Don't you know? Everything that tastes good is bad for you. Besides, it's not a Twinkie Twinkie," she adds, pointing at the dessert sushi.

"What is it? Like a Twinkie's bastard cousin? A Winkie Twinkie? A Kinky Twinkie?"

"It's a Trinkie," she says, laughing. "It's homemade. I whipped it up and brought it to the class. I made my own version of Twinkies. So they're not, y'know, disgusting. Here you go," she tells me.

I bite into the treat, and my eyes go wide. "Holy shit. You have to sell that."

"I'm so glad you like it," Josie says, with a grin. "And now you have done your due diligence as my favorite taste tester. Do you have any idea how awful it was for me when you were in Africa?"

"I can't even imagine the hell you went through without me around," I say, since I was gone for a year with Doctors Without Borders, doing a stint in the Central African Republic and helping out the people who've suffered most through the armed conflict and instability in that country. Those were some of the most challenging but also most gratifying times I've ever spent. It made me a better doctor; I hope it made me a better person, too.

It definitely made me miss Josie's taste tests of treats, though.

"It was rough, Chase," she says, all serious-looking as she teases me. "I just had to take it day by day to get through."

"Speaking of rough days . . . So this guy came into the ER earlier," I say, since Josie enjoys Tales from the ER. Her eyes light up, and she rubs her hands as if to say *tell me, tell me.* "He was testing the structural integrity of a chandelier," I say, then share the rest of the story of Aquaman's adventures.

She cringes, then laughs. "Well, that beats my crazy morning."

I narrow my eyes. "Don't tell me you tried to get intimate with a KitchenAid mixer?"

"Ha. No. Last week, I started looking for a roomie now that Natalie's moved out."

"Oh, yeah?" Natalie is Josie's former roommate. Now she's hitched to Wyatt and they're living together in his apartment.

"Talk about a pain in the forehead. This morning a woman who answered my ad stopped by to see my place and wanted to know my 'quiet hours.' Like, what time each night we have mandatory lights out at my home." Josie shoots me a look that tells me that's the nuttiest idea.

"Did you tell her the curfew at Chez Josie?"

"Nine p.m. On the dot," she says primly, straightening her spine. "But I didn't bother to tell her that after nine is when I go crazy and watch loud and naughty HBO shows."

"Like there's any other kind."

She taps my leg. "But that doesn't even compare to the lady who wanted to know if the building allowed snakes."

"No fucking way," I say, recoiling. I can handle blood, guts, and all manner of foreign objects in completely wrong locations, but animals that slither? Nope. Can't do it.

"Snakes. Why did it have to be snakes?" Josie and I ask in unison, quoting *Raiders of the Lost Ark*.

She shudders. "I swear looking for a roommate is all I've been doing, too. And the parade of crazy started as soon as I began advertising for a single female roommate, twenties to thirties. The *next* woman who answered the ad wanted to know if I would be baking at home. She said she was allergic to flour and feared my apartment would aggravate her sensitivities."

"See? I'm not sensitive at all. You could bake around me anytime."

"You could taste test everything I want to try making."

I puff up my cheeks. "I'd balloon out." I make a basketball arc over my stomach, too.

"Hardly." She darts out a hand and pats my belly. It's flat as a board. I work out a lot. Plus, I walk or bike all over the city. I like to stay busy. My mom said when I was a kid, I was a perpetual motion machine. She also called me high-energy, always on, and exasperating. And not necessarily in that order. But that's why medicine fits me so well, and that's also why I picked the ER for my practice. Keeps me on my toes, keeps me busy, keeps me moving. It's a mental and a physical challenge.

"If only you were a girl." Josie sighs dejectedly. "You'd be the perfect roommate."

"If only I were a girl, I'd play with my tits all day."

"You would not."

"Would so." I waggle my hands in front of my chest to mime my activity of choice in this *if only* scenario.

She swats me. "You're ridiculous." She tilts her head as a bird chirps in a nearby tree. "But enough about me. You must have good news on the apartment front by now. Did you get the place in Chelsea you were hoping for?"

I drag a hand through my hair. "Nope. And let's just say there were some conditions attached to the latest offer that made me realize I need to start from scratch. Mainly, my leasing agent pitched me a threesome."

Her jaw drops. "For real?"

I nod. "Yeah, for real. I'm confident it was a bona fide offer, since she told me she makes a great ceviche, too. Like, why else would you mention the ceviche? Clearly, she was using it as a lure."

Josie frowns. "I don't get it. Is ceviche like a thing in three-somes?"

I laugh, and shake my head. "No. Actually, I don't know because I'm not into that. But all I know is she was so god-damn normal about both the threesome and the fish dish, that's how I knew she was *for real*."

Josie holds up her hands in surrender. "You win. That's crazier than the curfew lady, the snake lady, or the no-baking lady."

"You're telling me. Bouncing around from place to place is wearing on me," I say with a sigh. When I'd returned to the United States a few months ago, I moved in with my brother Max, but he lives downtown—and I mean way downtown—and I work uptown. Besides, it's not my style to stay with him forever. "It's like I have some sort of curse when it comes to finding a decent rental. And you have a curse when it comes to finding—"

"A decent roommate." Her voice trails off as she stares at me. Really stares. And as she seems to study me, the answer clicks. The lightbulb literally goes off at the same time for both of us. I can see it in the sparkle in her eyes. I'm sure it matches mine.

"Why didn't we think of this before?" she asks slowly, as if she's inviting me to fill in the blanks.

I gesture from her to me. "You mean the fact that I can solve your roommate problem and you can solve my housing woes?"

She nods several times. "Just because I was originally looking for a female roommate doesn't mean . . ."

"That a male roommate wouldn't work out?" I offer, and a burst of hope rises in me. This could be the answer. Holy shit. This could be the motherfucking answer, and I won't have to give up a spleen, a kidney, or my love of one-on-one sex in exchange for polyamory.

She swallows. Looks nervous. "Would that be weird? I know you wanted a place to yourself."

I shake my head adamantly. "I just want *a place* at this point. Are you really offering?" I ask, and maybe I should consider all the fine details and nuances. But fuck, this isn't a patient presenting with unusual symptoms where I need to call in Dr. House. This is a simple malady. This is the headache with the take-aspirin-and-call-me-in-the-morning solution.

She holds out one hand like a scale, weighing the situation. "I need a roommate. I haven't found anyone who isn't crazy." Then the other hand. "You need somewhere to live. You haven't found any place that isn't cursed." She brushes her palms together. "And let's not forget we get along super well, and always have."

I nod vigorously. "We're like the poster children for getting along well."

"I mean, has there ever been a guy and a girl friend who get along as well as we do?"

I slash my hand through the air. "Fuck no. Not in the history of the world."

"Plus, you like my cooking, and I like your ability to not hog the bathroom mirror for a full hour when you dry your hair and do your makeup."

I gesture to my face. "In and out in under five. All-natural beauty here."

She nudges me with her elbow. "The other great thing is we'll each have our space. Since I work early we wouldn't be on top of each other every second."

My dick stirs, not because I'm horny for her, but hello? The image of her sweet, sexy body *on top of* me is legally required to induce an erection. If it didn't, I'd need to be tested for ED.

"We'd only be on top of each other a few seconds a day," I fire back, because that was too good to resist. Then, to sell myself more, because this is the golden ticket for both of us, I add, "I'm also amazingly good at reaching objects on tall shelves, opening champagne bottles, taking out the trash, and any other manly tasks you want to throw my way. Not to mention sewing up wounds and restarting hearts."

She taps a finger to her lips. "Manly tasks can be helpful. Plus, I have at least two dozen unopened champagne bottles crying out for your attention."

I pump a fist. "Does that mean you'll take that roommate ad down? Like, now?"

She grabs her phone and removes the ad. Like that, we take the aspirin to fix the problem, and we don't even need to call the doctor in the morning.

CHAPTER THREE

From the pages of Josie's Recipe Book

Josie's Swedish Fish Rolls

Ingredients

1 tablespoon butter

12 marshmallows

(But please, use the gelatin-free kind, because gelatin = gross. And as my friend Spencer says, beef candy is not a thing.)

2 cups puffed rice cereal

4 Fruit Roll-Ups

Swedish Fish

(The number of Swedish Fish is up to you. My rule of thumb is as many Swedish Fish as you need for the recipe, allowing for the fact that you will eat them as you make the sushi because Swedish Fish are delish.)

Directions

1. Melt butter in a medium saucepan over low heat and add marshmallows. Stir marshmallows until completely melted.

Speaking of melted, that's not at all how I feel around Chase Summers, no matter how good-looking he is. I swear that man does not melt me. He does, however, entertain me, and that's one of the many reasons I suggested we move in together. Living with Chase will be like having HBO on all day. Except, you know, minus the nudity. Unless I peek at him in the shower. And I'm totally not going to do that.

2. Add cereal and coat thoroughly.

3. Roll out the fruit roll-ups. Place 1/4 of the coated cereal onto each fruit roll-up and spread across.

4. Place a line of fish on the coated cereal.

5. Roll up the fruit roll-up with the crispy treat and the fish inside. Gently. Sushi candy needs a subtle, sensual touch.

6. Place a sharp knife into a bowl of very warm water. Slice. Serve.

7. Share with a friend.

Optional step: Pat self on back for having the most excellent idea of sharing an apartment with a good friend who makes you laugh and helps your business. We are such a great fit.

CHAPTER FOUR

Josie and I walk across town like two conquering generals who joined forces on the battlefield of New York real estate. Now we put the carnage behind us as we lay down the law of our new future.

Since she and Natalie took over a month-to-month lease from Charlotte when she moved out, we'll be paying some dude named Mr. Barnes. He owns the place, and Charlotte paved the way to transfer her lease when she left. Don't let anyone tell you New York real estate *isn't* about luck and who you know.

"I don't have a lot of rules, but I'll be frank. I don't like dirty socks, so please don't be a slob," Josie tells me as her sandals click on the sidewalk en route to her place in Murray Hill. Her short little skirt shows off her bare legs, toned from the soccer rec league she plays in. Even though I'm not checking out her legs. Her strong, shapely legs.

I scoff. "I'm basically the neatest guy around."

She gives me a side-eyed stare. "And you're straight?"

I hold up my hands. "Woman, straight men can be clean. Do not stereotype."

She laughs and elbows my side as we stroll east. "I'm teasing. I know both things about you. Your straightness and your cleanliness, Doctor McHottie," she says as we pass a flower shop. The nickname nearly halts me in my tracks, but before I can ask why she called me that, and if she does really think of me that way, she's moved on to a new topic. "As for music, noise, TV, and all that jazz, all I ask is we be respectful of each other. I do wake up early to open the bakery, and I need a solid seven hours of sleep or I'm a total witch."

"You? A witch? I doubt it."

She cackles and curves her fingers into claws. "Complete with the pointy hat and black cat if I don't sleep well."

"I won't disturb your slumber with heavy metal, or playing my audiobooks out loud," I say as we reach the crosswalk and wait for the little man in the sign to turn green. "Besides, I'm all about the earphones, anyway. My relationship with my headphones is quite possibly the longest one I've had."

That trumps the year-long one with my ex, a fellow doctor named Adele, and even that lasted about eleven months longer than it should have. A dark cloud hovers at the edge of my thoughts; I don't like thinking about the girl who was my closest friend once upon a time. I basically try to never think of Adele, if I can help it.

"We're on the same page about hours, cleanliness, and cooking, and our schedules fit well together," Josie says, as we separate briefly to give room to a harried mom charging through the evening crowds with a stroller. "Oh, and rent is due on the first of the month to Mr. Barnes, and if you want to move in right away, that would be awesome." She seems a little guilty, like maybe she feels bad asking me to move in so soon. But hell, I'm effectively a homeless guy, so her speed-is-of-the-essence offer sounds good.

"I can be in this weekend," I say.

"Thank God," she says, exhaling deeply. "I have to admit, I took out a loan a few months ago to expand the bakery, and I've been stretched a bit thin between payments and rent each month. It's doable, but I just really need a roomie to spread the cost. That's why I'm so glad you can do this. You're saving me. I don't know what I'd do without you stepping up like this."

I squeeze her shoulder. "You can count on me, Josie. I've got a year-long contract at Mercy, so I'm not skipping town. And besides, you're saving me, so we're totally even."

"Good. I need you for even more than your talented mouth now," she says, and I blink and stare at her, trying to figure out if she's even aware of the innuendo that just spilled from her pretty lips. But she's about to be.

I wiggle my eyebrows. "My mouth is damn talented. And did you know my tongue has amazing stamina?"

Rolling her eyes, she chuckles. "I deserved that. I left you no choice but to go there."

I nod. "You can't say things like that and expect me not to comment."

"Oh, believe you me, I know about your level of dirty commentary, and it's a damn good thing I find it amusing. And all your naughty comments are making me forget the tips and guidelines for roommate compatibility that I'm supposed to review." She stops in front of a tall stone church with a slate gray exterior, gazing up at the vast New York sky, a rare cloudless blue this evening as the sun dips toward the horizon. She looks as if she's contemplating something, but then she shrugs happily. "I had this whole list of questions to ask potential roommates, but it doesn't really matter anymore. I know we're compatible."

I hold my arms out wide. "I'm easy. What you see is what you get."

"You know I love that about you," she says as we resume our pace across town.

We've known each other for years, and Josie and I hit it off from day one. When I visited her parents' home in New York City with Wyatt during my junior year of college, we clicked instantly. The first time I walked through the door of the family's brownstone on the Upper West Side, she didn't even hesitate to throw her arms around me and welcome me into the home. After that embrace, she thrusted a plate of mini cupcakes at me, and the rest was history.

She was home from college at the same time as I was, and one of the reasons we got along so well is we're close in age. I skipped two grades as a kid, so I wound up starting college at sixteen. Wyatt and I were in the same graduating class at school, but he's two years older. Anyway, I went on to spend many weekends at Wyatt's home since my folks live outside Seattle and I attended school near Manhattan. Along with Wyatt's twin brother, Nick, we all hung out together on those long weekends, watching movies and traipsing around the city checking out bands and visiting—ironically, of course— tourist traps like the wax museum in Times Square to photo- bomb as many pictures as possible.

At the clubs, Nick and Wyatt gave Josie and me a hard time because we weren't old enough to drink. In our favor, though, we discovered we made a powerful Scrabble team, and we crushed the Hammer twins in our games. I knew the killer science words like "dyspnea" and "zygosity," and Josie, the lit major, slayed it with her all-around love of words, including her mastery of the two-letter Scrabble ones. We destroyed those fuckers one night in a nine-letter game with a one-two punch of "diplococci" and "Qi."

The prize?

They had to go out and buy us beer. Victory had never tasted so good.

Funny that even though Wyatt's my buddy, I've managed to become close friends with his sister, too. Probably helps that Wyatt knows there's nothing cooking between Josie and me. Hell, how else do you explain being friends with a girl this long? Obviously, I don't want her.

Besides, I've been there and learned the hard way that getting into a relationship with a woman you're friends with can only end in heartbreak. Thank you, Adele, for that little lesson. I won't go there again. Ever.

When we reach Fifth Avenue, Josie clears her throat, returning me to the moment. "But there is one thing I want to ask from my list of roommate questions."

"Hit me with it."

"What's your romantic situation? That's just something that's good to know for two people about to live together, don't you think?"

Her eyes meet mine. The question strikes me as odd. Doesn't she know my romantic situation? "I'm not involved with anyone. But you knew that."

She holds up her hands, almost defensively. "I didn't want to assume anything. You might have met a pretty young thing last night," she says lightly.

I laugh. "Nope. Last night I rode twenty-five miles with Max after work. Prep for the century we're doing at the end of the summer." I raise my chin toward her, then something sticks in my throat as I force out, "Are you? Involved with someone romantically?"

Why does it sound like I'm croaking? And why am I clenching my fists, hoping to hell she'll say no?

She shakes her head as we cross the avenue and head toward her pad. I haven't seen her place before, but I know where she lives in the city. She moved when I was in Africa. "Nope."

I breathe a strange sigh of relief. Then I tell myself it's just easier if whoever I live with is unentangled. Significant others can be ballbreakers, no matter the gender. "Cool," I say, keeping my tone light.

"But I've started online dating."

My stomach twists. "Why would you do that?"

She gives me a look as if I'm crazy for asking. "Why wouldn't I? I'm twenty-eight and single in the city. I wouldn't mind meeting a nice guy."

"And you think you'll meet him online? A pretty young thing?"

"Why not? That's how people meet these days." She gestures to me. "Where do you meet women?"

Most of the women I've been involved with in my late twenties have been doctors or nurses, to be honest, or chicks I met at a bar and banged. Hey, it happens. I don't say all that to Josie, though.

"Work, usually. That's where I meet people." I rub a hand over my jaw, processing what online dating might mean. "Are you going to bring home some dude you meet online?"

She laughs. "You said that as if it tasted like vinegar."

It kind of did. Truthfully, I hadn't noodled on this part of the roommate equation. While I didn't think either one of us would monk it up and practice celibacy, I hadn't factored in the impact of another person's love life, either. Shit, now I need to think about the nuances of her bringing dudes home. Like finding a sock on the doorknob when I get off work. That image doesn't sit well with me. "Will there be a tube sock to warn me to stay away?"

She winks. "No, a sexy black lace thong."

I nearly stumble on a sidewalk crack. She'd look good in a black thong. She'd look good in a pink one. A white one. Any color. Oh fuck, and soon she might even walk around the apartment in just—

"And for the record, I do not strut around the apartment wearing nothing but heels and underwear."

Damn. There goes that dream. But maybe I can resurrect it. "Any chance you'd consider making that fashion statement? Say, in about three days, once I move in?"

She laughs as she shakes her head. "I don't think either one of us wants to be caught with our pants down. Let's be honest. I was looking for a female roommate because it's just easier for a woman to live with a woman. Same reason you were looking for your own place. But neither one of us had any luck. Now, we just have to be thoughtful and considerate of the fact that we're a man and a woman who are good friends living together, and we'll have to adjust to things like the other person dating, and me possibly bringing home a guy or you potentially bringing home a girl, right?"

I nod. She's right, even though I wish she weren't. And while it's not like I was hitting it and quitting it every single night, something about bringing a woman home to a place I'll share with Josie seems . . . odd. Even so, it's best to be prepared. "Yeah, we'll need a plan."

"Exactly."

"Should we just do what any good roommate does? Screw someone in the bathroom at a bar before we go home?" I suggest innocently, batting my eyes.

She swats my arm as we cross the street. "You're terrible. I simply mean that we'll need a code word. A heads-up. I'll text you, or you'll text me with that word."

"Like aardvark? I've always thought aardvark would be an awesome code word because it's completely obvious it's a code word."

She calls me on my bluff, narrowing her eyes as we reach the block with her building. "Aardvark it is. But what if things get awkward between us?"

"What would be awkward between us?"

She shrugs. "I don't know. Like maybe if you're showering when I come home, how will I know to stay out of the bathroom?"

I furrow my brow. "Wouldn't the sound of the shower be all you need to stay out?"

She snaps her fingers. "Good point. I guess I was just thinking . . . if anything felt awkward between us . . ." She waves her hand from her to me and back.

Ohhhhhh.

I get it now.

I pretend to whisper. "You mean," I say, taking my time to drawl out each syllable, "sex-u-al ten-sion?"

Her cheeks flush. "No. I just mean awkward. I don't mean *that*. Just that we're a man and a woman living together. It's just smart to be prepared for any . . . weirdness."

"Just kidding, Josie," I say, and drape an arm around her. "Things will never be awkward between us. But if they ever get that way, just say 'Swedish Fish.' That will be our safe word."

"But then how do we defuse the tension?"

I tap my chin. "That's a very good question."

Neither one of us has an answer.

A few minutes later, we enter her building, head to the elevator, and shoot up six floors. As we walk down the hall, she gives me her preamble. "Both rooms are tiny. When Charlotte moved out to live with Spencer, Mr. Barnes gave approval so that we could have Wyatt turn the one-bedroom apartment into two bedrooms so Natalie and I could live here."

She unlocks the door, guides me through the living room, and swings open the entrance to my new bedroom.

My eyebrows shoot into my hairline. It's the size of . . . well, of a mattress. The bed is up against the wall, and if the other room is the same size as this one, that means my bed will be next to her bed.

One thin wall will separate us.

Talk about Swedish Fish.

CHAPTER FIVE

My brother's laughter booms across all of Battery Park as he greases the chain on his bike. A streetlamp illuminates his work. Morning hints at the horizon, but the sky is still the dark blue before the dawn. It's five-thirty on a Friday, and we're getting ready to ride.

I adjust the tire pressure on my bike as I jerk my head to look at Max. "What's so funny?"

He wipes down the chain with a rag, making sure it's well-oiled. "What you just said. That's what is funny."

"That I'm moving in with Josie?"

He nods several times. "Yup. That one. And I thought you were the genius in the family. But you must have forgotten to take a dose of common sense the other day," he says as he spins the chain.

Max builds custom cars for a living, so this kind of pre-ride prep is part of his rule book. Besides, today's training calls for thirty miles, and we want to make sure the two-wheelers can handle that. With this century ride coming up soon, we need to be ready. Hence the early morning start. We're on a team that's raising money for better medical care for veterans.

I stand, resting a palm on the seat of my road bike. "This choice is one hundred percent common sense. We've been friends forever, and we both need a place to live. Besides, you kicked me out."

Max stands, too, rising to his full height. I'm a tall guy, but he's taller than my six feet, and broader. He's basically the definition of intimidating, especially when you add in the big muscles and the dark eyes. But he's a total teddy bear to me and always has been, so the big hulking look doesn't work.

He points at my chest. "I did not kick you out. I told you that you were welcome to stay in the lap of older brother luxury as long as you wanted," he says, gesturing behind him to the sweet-as-sin high-rise building he lives in. I already rode a few miles downtown to meet him here.

"Nah. Too far from Mercy. Josie's closer. Only takes me ten minutes to get to work from her place, instead of thirty from here."

He claps a hand on my shoulder. "I hardly think the extra twenty minutes each way is worth you shacking up with a girl you're hot for, man. That's crazy."

I scoff. "I'm not hot for Josie. I've been friends with her forever."

He fixes me with a steely stare. Fine, he's not all teddy bear. Sometimes he's a hard ass, like when he tries to give me his serious eyes. "Do you or do you not think she's hot?"

I raise my chin. I can hold my own under his inquisition. Besides, the answer is as easy as pie. A delicious cherry pie, like the one Josie made for me a few weeks ago. "I do think she's hot." He smirks, but I hold up a finger to correct him. "On a purely scientific, empirical basis."

He shakes his head like he doesn't believe me.

"Let the record reflect I have never done a damn thing about it. And that's because I'm highly evolved. I can admire a woman's appearance without wanting to get in her pants."

Max claps me on the back. "Then I hope you and your purely scientific appreciation of Josie's physical attributes have no problem being in such close proximity to all those empirical assets of hers," he says, grabbing the helmet from the handlebars and snapping it on with one hand. He straddles his bike.

I mount mine, too. "Why do you think I can't handle living with her? I like her. She's awesome."

His laughter answers me again. "Because you flirt with her incessantly."

We pedal away from the park, heading toward the Hudson River Greenway with a handful of other early-morning cyclists.

"And yet, I have somehow amazingly never come on to her. Don't you think if I was attracted to her, something would have happened at least once in all the years I've known her?"

He shakes his head as we pick up speed, riding side by side on the path now. "No. Because now you're kicking it up a notch, and there's this thing that happens when you pour gasoline on something and then light a match."

"Oh yeah?" I adopt a simpleton tone. "What's that thing that happens? Does it . . . I dunno . . . catch fire?"

He snorts. "I would smack you upside the head if we weren't on bikes right now." Our wheels turn faster as we sail over the smooth concrete path, swerving carefully around joggers and power-walkers.

As we pass a pack of runners, I pull ahead. "I bet you would," I call out. "If you could catch me."

I spend all of the next thirty miles maintaining a pace that's a couple of bike lengths ahead of my big brother. When we're done, my heart beats fast, and sweat slides down my forehead. I dismount where we started, in Battery Park, and he does the same.

I glance at my watch. "Just enough time for a hearty breakfast before work." I've got an hour until I'm due at Mercy for my shift. Fridays tend to be busy days at the ER. The action heats up, especially on a Friday afternoon. This might be my only meal today.

"Let's do it."

"Oh, and by the way, that's exactly how I'll manage living with Josie—like I did staying ahead of you the whole ride. I'll just keep pace ahead of any potential complications," I say, as we make our way to our favorite diner right across the street.

"Keep telling yourself that." We lock up our bikes, and head inside to order.

And that's exactly what I'll tell myself when I move in this weekend.

CHAPTER SIX

I point to the curved wooden stand with a hook at the top. "This. Explain this."

Josie sets her hands on her hips. "It's a banana holder."

I give her a stern look. "I can read. I don't need to know *what*. I need to know *why*." I poke the object on the shelf at Bed Bath & Beyond, otherwise known as the Nexus of Unnecessary Things. Pretty sure there's some kind of vortex or force field right smack dab in the middle of this store attracting all the weird, bizarre, and odd home goods. "Why can't they sit on the kitchen counter? Or, how about in a bowl?"

"Maybe the bananas just like to dangle?" she suggests. "Hang free and all?"

Smacking my forehead, I go along with it. "Aha. That makes perfect sense."

"I'm here to help." She tugs on my shirtsleeve. "But can we please get to the sheet aisle? You can't sleep on a naked mattress."

"That may be true, but I could definitely sleep naked on a mattress," I offer, and she laughs as we navigate through another sardine-packed aisle in the mammoth store.

It's one in the afternoon, and I just moved in this morning. That took all of two hours. Spending my twenties in med school and as a resident gave me very little time for the acquisition of things, so most of my possessions fit in a duffel bag. I have very little. Not even sheets for a queen-size bed. Ergo, I'm spending Saturday at Bed Bath & Beyond, which is a bit like wandering through a Buzzfeed post titled "Ten Things I'll Never Use."

More like five hundred. Wait. Make that five hundred and one, because I just spotted the new number one item on the list.

"That," I say as I make a beeline for a shelf of crème brûlée torches. Grabbing a silvery one, I hold it up. "Please say we can have a housewarming party, and you'll make crème brûlée, and I can stride all proud and awesome into the kitchen," I say, puffing out my chest and deepening my voice. "And I can light it with a torch, and we'll all *ooh* and *ahh* at the manly fire I made when I lit up a dessert."

She arches an eyebrow. "A manly fire?"

I nod vigorously. "And then you'll let the guests take turns punching me in the face for being a total douche for owning a crème brûlée torch."

She narrows her eyes. "You actually want people to punch you?"

I'm deadly serious as I answer her. "If I ever own a crème brûlée torch, you have carte blanche to punch me, Josie. You really should." I drop the torch on the shelf and take her hand, clasping it tightly in mine. "Promise me. From this day forward. Promise you'll punch me if I ever own a crème brûlée torch, a rotating tie rack, or more than one kind of cheese grater. This is part of our roommate pact."

She grips my hand tighter, her green eyes glowing with stark seriousness. "I solemnly swear to pummel you under all the aforementioned circumstances. As proof of our friendship and roommate solidarity."

"You're a saint," I say, then wrap a hand around her head and tug her close for a quick kiss on her forehead.

And hello, sweet, sexy scent of Josie. What is this delicious smell? Is it . . . oh fuck me. *Cherries.* My God, she smells like cherries. Like the perfect summer fruit. Like the naughtiest fruit. And I've got to wonder if that cherry scent is her face lotion, her shampoo, or her body wash?

Body wash.

My mind is adrift, and the word association begins. Because what goes with body wash but nudity?

Naked woman in the shower. Washing. Lathering. Soaping.

Ah, hell.

Snap the fuck out it, Summers.

I stuff those images into a far corner in the dark closet of my mind and pull back from Josie, leaving the questions unanswered. I slap on a happy, wholesome smile. "Thank you for your commitment to my non-douchery endeavors."

"I've got your back," she says, and pats me.

Then she points to a cupcake tin. She pants like a dog. "Must. Have."

"Don't you have twenty of those?"

She nods as she grabs it from a shelf. "Yes. But I need more." She spins around, and her hand darts out for something else. "It's an icing smoother. I need a new one. Gah, this aisle is like baker porn." She smiles gleefully.

"Baker porn. I like that," I say, then offer to hold the kitchen goods. She hands them to me, and I tuck them under my arm.

When we turn the corner toward the next aisle, Josie stops at the end cap. She taps on a big silvery box. "Quick. Waffle maker. This is the true test of our roommate compatibility. Do you need a waffle maker?"

I peer at her through narrowed eyes, then slam my free hand as if I'm hitting a buzzer on a game show. "And the correct answer is: No. Never. That's what Sunday brunch is for."

She holds up a palm and we smack hands. "You win this round of the New Roommate Show. Because who wants to buy a monstrosity for the kitchen counter to make waffles in once a year and then have no place to put it in our tiny New York apartment?"

"Not this guy."

"And not this girl."

Damn, we rock at living together.

We soldier on through the store.

On our quest for sheets, we wander through sconces. And seriously, what the fuck is a sconce? Does anyone even know what a sconce is? No, no one does, because it's not a thing. Then an entire rack of high-end ice cream makers, which forces me to ask—who the hell decided we should make our own ice cream? Have people, I dunno, not heard of Talenti's, Edy's, Ben and Jerry's, or the corner ice cream shop?

At the end of a maze of aisles and escalators, we arrive at the sheets. I blink and stare. Up and up and up. "Josie, there are literally five hundred kinds of sheets here," I say, my tone heavy.

"Choice is good," she says, tapping her finger on her chin as she checks out the options.

I survey the rows upon rows of navy, black, white, dotted, and other manly-patterned sheets, and immediately I'm overwhelmed. Why is sheet shopping so complicated? I swear restarting a heart is easier than figuring out the proper thread count.

I gesture to the mountains of Egyptian cotton. "But each one says it's better than the last. What happens if I get the soft three hundred? Will I wonder if the five hundred was the softest after all? And is bigger better? Do I need the eight hundred? How do I decide?"

She grabs a packet of four hundred thread count sheets and thrusts it in my arms with an authority that's downright . . . hot. "That's how you do it."

"Damn, woman. You just made the decision like that." I snap my fingers.

"You can't go wrong with white sheets. And they'll be just the right amount of soft," she says, stroking the plastic cover of the sheets. My eyes drift to her fingers, and I stare as she runs them down the cover of the sheets. My mind leapfrogs several inappropriate paces ahead to how her fingers might feel running down my abs . . . Or if her belly is just the right amount of soft . . .

I shake my head. Of course she's the right amount of soft. She should be soft. Women are usually soft—that's just a simple fact.

"I'm sold," I say, tucking the sheets under my arm with the rest of our haul and ferrying her away from the bed supplies lest any more errant fantasies pop into my head thanks to the free association of Josie, sheets, fingers, stroking, soft skin, cherries, or any fucking other thing.

As we leave this section, she stops at a giant tub of velvety pillows of all shapes and sizes. "I need a new pillow."

I frown in confusion. "For what?"

She grabs a royal blue pillow with sequins on the edges and clutches it to her chest. "I like pillows."

"Are you a pillow-phile?"

"Total pillow-phile." Dropping the blue one in the vat, she dips her hand in and riffles around, rooting through a sea of chocolate brown, deep purple, and rich red pillows. Some are square, some circular, some cylindrical. She finds one that's emerald green and long.

"Look!" Her face lights up as if she's discovered a pirate's booty.

"What's the pillow love all about, Josie?"

Hugging it tighter, she answers, "Pillows are wonderful. We can nap with them, cuddle with them, put our feet on them. Also," she says, wagging a finger to draw me closer and dropping her voice to a whisper, "they're boob friends."

And I'm a cartoon character knocked senseless. It's as if I've been hit with a frying pan of naughty, and the dirty lobe of my brain has rattled free. "Boob friends?"

Josie wiggles her eyebrows and backs up into the aisle next to the pillows.

I follow.

I'd follow her anywhere right now because she just uttered my favorite word. *Boobs.* For the record, my second favorite word is tits. Third is breasts.

She bites her lip, glances from side to side, then draws the pillow right between the valley of the goddesses on her chest.

I groan.

Audibly.

And my dick springs to attention in my jeans, the shameless fucker.

Then, it's story time for Josie Hammer, as she launches into a tale. "Once upon a time, I had a stuffed crocodile. He was a small, green creature who lived on my bed, a present from when I was younger and in the middle of a big love fest for the *Lyle, Lyle, Crocodile* books. I made him talk, and I named him Lyle Lyle, too."

"Clever."

Her eyes twinkle. "But what was truly clever was how in middle school I discovered Lyle Lyle's real purpose. You see, he came in quite handy for this early bloomer. When I was twelve and started getting these," she says, gesturing to those absolutely fucking magnificent globes, "I started sleeping with Lyle Lyle."

"You slept with the stuffed crocodile?" I ask, my throat as dry as my dick is hard.

She nods and hugs the green pillow tighter between her breasts.

"Why did you sleep with him?" I ask because the answer eludes me.

She shifts her weight so she's leaning a bit to the right. "Because when you sleep on your side, the girls kind of fall on top of each other and smash each other. It can be a little un-comfortable."

Yeah, like the tightness in my pants right now.

"I bet," I choke out.

"So Lyle Lyle got a job. I enlisted him as a boob friend. I slept with him every night, and he delivered complete and utter boob comfort."

That lucky fucking inanimate animal. "I want to grow up to be a stuffed crocodile."

Josie's green eyes widen, then she laughs. "I like you just fine as you, though."

I hold up my forearm. "Then consider this. Would this work as a boob friend? Hypothetically, of course. I'm pretty sure my hand would fit nicely between a pair of boobs."

She swats me. "If the pillow fails, I'll rap twice on the wall."

"Honestly, you don't even have to knock. Just come into my room, grab my hand, and slide it between the girls." My eyes drift to her 36Cs. What? I can tell from looking. It's a scientific gift of mine.

"What color are my eyes?"

Her question doesn't compute. I snap my gaze back up to her face. "Green."

She points to the bridge of her nose. "And they're here."

"Seriously? You were talking about boobs. Pragmatically speaking, I had no choice but to look at the topic of conversation."

She gives me an I-caught-you stare.

I hold up my hands. "This is not a Swedish Fish moment. You brought it up."

She lifts the green pillow and bonks me on the head with it. "And your hand offer is noted."

"Just trying to be helpful. That's all."

"And I appreciate it. I'm also buying this pillow."

When we reach the counter, I pay for the pillow and hand it to her. I pay for her baking goods, too. "Have I ever told you I give amazing gifts? It's kind of a special talent of mine."

She rolls her eyes, but as we leave, she lets go of the teasing and drops a soft kiss on my cheek. "Thank you for the amazing gifts. That was very sweet of you."

Later, as we spend our first night together as roommates, I'm weirdly jealous of a pillow.

But a week or so after that, it's not pillows I'm jealous of.

CHAPTER SEVEN
From the pages of Josie's Recipe Book

Air-Popped Popcorn for Nights Hanging Out on the Couch

Ingredients

1/4 cup unpopped corn kernels

One popcorn popper

Directions

1. Place the kernels in the popcorn popper.

2. Put the top on.

3. Stick that baby in the microwave.

4. This is the toughest part. Gather close. Wait for it . . . hit the popcorn button on the microwave. Watch it. When the microwave dings, voila!

Serving suggestion: Dump the popped corn into a bowl, sprinkle with a little salt, grate a small bit of parmesan cheese, and prepare to enjoy the hell out of a snack as you curl up on the couch and watch TV.

Special instructions: Resist placing your feet on Chase's legs. Refrain from snuggling up next to him. Keep your hands out of that hair. That golden brown, slightly wavy, looks-so-damn-soft hair. You are friends, and you like hanging out with him. It's that simple, and don't presume that friendship means you get the chance to touch his hair. Even though you really, really, *really* want to touch his hair.

CHAPTER EIGHT

Six things I've learned about women from living with one. . .

One

They use a lot of toilet paper.

Okay, hold on. I don't mean anything untoward. What I mean is this—it's like an epic fiesta of tissue in the bathroom.

"Can you pick up TP on your way home?" Josie asks on the phone one evening as I'm leaving the hospital after an insane day of sprains and broken bones. "We're almost out."

"There's half a roll," I say, because that's good for three days, right?

Nope.

I'm wrong.

"Chase," she chides as I head down the street. "That'll be gone in a couple of hours."

And I know why. The chick loves toilet paper. She's like one of those cat memes, where the pussycat's paws are wrapped around the roll, and she's gleefully tugging it off the holder. Josie uses it for everything.

She uses it to take off her makeup. She uses it to clean up water on the bathroom sink. She uses it to *dust*. Yup, she wads up a chunk of TP and wipes down the shelves with it. She fucking unravels it with her little feline paws. She uses it when she blows her nose, which, incidentally, is kind of adorable since she makes a little squeak.

I pop into the drugstore and grab some TP. I get her favorite kind. Because it makes her happy.

Two

Hair.

It's pretty much everywhere. I find brown strands on the couch. I discover pink strands in the sink. And, truth be told, I find Josie's hair in my own hair. Shhh. Don't tell her but . . . I use her hairbrush. I don't know why, but girls' brushes are evidently way better than combs. They're just really fucking awesome.

Three

Josie really likes it when I perform manly tasks. I like it when she likes it when I do manly tasks. Sorry if that makes me not PC or whatever. I'm sure I should be defying stereotypical gender roles and knitting her a scarf or planting flowers, but I won't lie—I vastly prefer when she asks me to lift shit. A few days ago, she wanted to move the coffee table. I happily obliged, and I enjoyed the fact that she checked out my arms when I carried it. The other night, she asked me to open a pickle jar. I strutted into the kitchen, flexed my arms, and made a big show of it.

"Peacock," she muttered.

I wiggled my eyebrows. "It's really hard to sound like you're insulting me when you say that word."

She rolled her eyes. "Ding dong."

I shrugged. "Again, not insulted."

"Pickle-jar-opening show-off."

I tapped her nose. "Bingo."

"You're insulted now?" She pumped a fist. "Excellent."

I frowned. "You're trying to insult me. I'm so sad," I said, then I reached into the jar and ate a pickle.

She patted my belly. "Pregnant?"

I shuddered. "Horrors."

"Oh, please. Like that's the worst thing in the world."

I gave her a sharp stare. "It kind of would be."

I'd rather be firing the trigger on the baby, not carrying it.

Like I said, I prefer manly tasks.

Four

After a long day at the hospital, which pretty much describes every day at Mercy, it's nice to have someone to come home to. And I'm not just saying that because Josie makes absolutely killer air-popped popcorn.

But she does. This popcorn is delicious, and we munch on it all the way through a binge fest of *Ballers*, *Vice Principals*, and *Veep* on HBO. When we reach the end, I rattle the bowl then pretend to hunt for more, sniffing the inside of it.

"You're like a dog," she says. "The dog who licks his food dish when he finishes just in case there's a nugget he missed."

I drop my face into the red bowl and lick.

She grabs it from me and sets it on the coffee table. "I'm cutting you off." She puts her feet on the coffee table. Then she shifts a little and moves them onto me.

I stare at her feet. Her toenails are painted sapphire blue. Her feet are little and slender. My eyes land on the top of her foot, and they nearly pop out of my head when I spy the bounty. "You have really beautiful veins in your feet."

She gives me the biggest side-eye glare in the world. "What?"

I stretch forward, grab her foot, and hold it up. "Look at this. It's fucking beautiful," I say, running my finger along the top. The vein there is thick and blue. "I could draw so much blood from here."

She blinks. "Are you a vampire?"

"No. I'm just an aficionado of all the systems in the body. You could give blood from your fucking foot." I yank it toward my mouth.

She squeals, wriggling as I pretend to gnaw on her arch. "You're crazy."

I let go, dropping it across my thigh. "What other glorious life-giving veins are you hiding? Let me see your arms."

"Is this some kind of doctor porn?"

I nod, and my eyes are surely sparkling. "You have the cupcake tin and icing smoother. Hell, I saw the way you eyed that rolling pin, too. You had your fun. Let me have mine."

"Fine." She shrugs off a little flimsy sweater and sticks out her arm.

I wrap my hand around her wrist and roam my eyes up and down her arm. "This," I say, tapping a vein in her forearm. "You could save countries with this limb."

"Are you really serious?"

"Yes. This is a world-class vein, Josie. This is like a diamond mine. Man, if I didn't already think you were the cat's meow, just seeing your veins would seal the deal. Please tell me you're a blood donor."

She nods. "Of course. Want to take mine some time?"

I draw a sharp breath and close my eyes. "Don't get me excited."

When I open my eyes, she kicks me in the belly. "You're the worst."

"I know."

She sits up and asks, "What was the hardest part about being in Africa?"

"Besides missing pizza?"

She smiles. "Besides pizza, though I do understand that kind of empty ache."

"Especially for a cheese pie with mushrooms."

"Your favorite," she says.

Absently, I rub my hand over her arm as I cycle back to the days in the Central African Republic. "Obviously, the suffering that we witnessed."

"Of course," she says, her tone serious. "That must have been so hard."

"It was. But on a more personal level, since I think that's what you're asking, I would say it was missing friends," I say with a sigh. "I missed Max, even though he's a pain, and Wyatt, too. I missed talking to friends who aren't in medicine. Just chatting about something other than work or doctor stuff."

"You're a social person," she says, her voice soft.

I nod. "Always have been. I loved your emails, though," I say, remembering how Josie kept in touch with me. She consistently sent me updates, more than anyone else. "I'd get excited just seeing your name in my Gmail inbox."

She smiles widely. "Really?"

I nod. "Yeah. It was an amazing experience being there, but I did miss home, and getting your notes was like receiving a little piece of New York every time you wrote. Like the time you told me about the woman who ordered a cake for herself from her dogs. How when she picked it up, she said, 'My dogs ordered me a cake.'"

Josie laughs. "She was adorable. She was a writer. She'd just hit a bestseller list, and she said her dogs wanted to congratulate her with a cake."

"What a lovable nut. And you totally went along with it."

Josie juts up a shoulder. "Of course. I said, 'Satchel and Lulu are so very proud of you. Here's the chocolate layer cake they ordered just for you.'"

"You probably made her day. Hell, that story alone made mine. What didn't help was the picture you sent along of the cake, you temptress," I say, narrowing my eyes.

"You missed my cake. So sweet."

A smile tugs at my lips. A wistful one. "I missed you, too."

"You did?" she asks, her voice softer than usual, less teasing.

"Of course. You're one of my best friends."

"Right. Totally. Same here." She clears her throat. "Did you make new friends in Africa?"

"Definitely. I became friends with some of the other doctors and nurses."

"Nurses?" A tightness threads through her voice. I haven't heard that tone before. For a flicker of a second it sounds almost like jealousy. But that's ridiculous. We've been friends for too long for things to change between us.

"A group of us became close. Camila, this hip nurse from Spain with crazy tattoos down her arms, was awesome."

"A Spanish nurse? Covered in ink?" she asks, like this is the most difficult concept, or the most annoying.

"Yes. She was a riot. Always telling funny stories about the guys back home. And a doctor from England, George. And another doc from New Zealand. His name was Dominic, and he had the perfect deadpan sense of humor. That was our crew."

"Did anyone have a vein fetish like you?"

I wiggle my eyebrows. "They would have if a specimen such as yourself had been around to provide doctor porn," I say, and grab her arm again, running my finger along her vein as if I'm mesmerized.

For a brief second, her breath catches. The soft, barely-there hair on her arm stands on end. A strange sensation runs down my spine, as if I'm floating.

Which makes no sense, so I shove the idea away.

I look away from her arm and meet her green eyes. There's something different in them. Something I haven't seen before. I don't know what it is. I can't name it.

"I've been using your hairbrush," I blurt out. I'm not entirely sure why I'm confessing right now, but here, with those wide eyes staring into mine, I can't help myself.

Her mouth lifts. "I know."

"You don't mind?"

She leans forward and runs a hand through my hair. That strange feeling? It doubles. It triples. It multiples exponentially. "No. But I think you'd look nice with pink hair someday."

Five

The smells.

The other thing about living with a woman is that everything smells good. The bathroom is like an opium den of feminine delights. Most days, Josie wakes up before me and leaves right when I rise. When I enter the bathroom, it's like wandering into a lair of womanhood.

I stand and inhale.

Cherry scents and swirling aromas of vanilla sugar lotion and honeysuckle body wash linger in the air, like a fucking delicious dirty dream. Every morning, I'm enrobed in the scent of woman. It's sweet and seductive and intoxicating, and it smells like her.

In short, it's the fucking perfect environment for a shower jerk.

What? Do you blame me? I wake up with wood, and I'm alone under a hot stream. Of course I do some morning handiwork.

Six

That's the other thing about living with a woman that a man just has to battle. Something he can't avoid.

Morning wood.

Waking up with a hard-on is a fact of having a Y chromosome. Most of the time Josie's gone before I even leave for work, so who cares? But, every now and then she's not. Like on Saturday morning. Clad only in black boxer briefs, I pad out of my room, rubbing my eyes and yawning. There she is in the hallway wearing the most adorable little pair of pink boy shorts that do nothing to reduce the tent in my pants. In fact, the view of her soft thighs and the swell of her tits under that flimsy T-shirt material enhances the outline in my shorts to completely fucking obvious levels.

Because . . .

She's. Not. Wearing. A. Bra.

I'm not a religious man, but I'm seriously considering taking up praying. To her chest. I think this is what heaven looks like. Those globes. God help me, I'm seeing an angel in front of me.

"Morning, Chase."

"Morning, Josie," I say, my voice gravelly from the hour and the view.

Her eyes drift down, and she blinks. My gaze follows hers, and my dick is pointing at her, like a happy billboard.

She doesn't seem fazed.

I shrug. "I meant, it's a very good morning indeed."

Josie smirks, and I can't help but notice she stares a little longer than one would expect. Can't say that bothers me.

But that night isn't so good at all when I learn the thing that sucks most about having a female roommate like Josie.

She's going on a date.

Chapter Nine

I try to leave before she does.

I don't want to know what she's wearing. I don't want to know how she does her hair. I don't even want to know where she's going.

Until she tells me. My hand is on the doorknob, ready to hightail it out of the apartment, since I can't be the pathetic ass who's home when his fuck-hot roommate heads out on a date.

Josie calls out to me from the hallway. "Hey!"

"Yeah?"

She walks into the living room. "I'm going to Bar Boisterous in the Fifties."

I narrow my eyes. "Okay. Why are you telling me?"

"So you'll know where my last-known location is."

Annoyance threads through me. "Please don't tell me you're going out with someone you think is going to dismember you."

She shudders and wags spooky fingers. "Yes. I'll have him send my head to you in a box."

"Not funny."

"What if he puts a bow on top? Like a gift?" She steps closer and adopts a Vincent Price narrator style. "He's going to cut me up in tiny pieces and feed me to the wolverines."

"Seriously. Not funny. Are you really worried about this guy?" I ask, not giving in to her attempt at humor. Though, in all other circumstances, Josie wins major points for being not just a humor consumer, but a humor producer. And that's rare. Humor producers are diamonds.

Just not this second.

She parks her hands on her hips. She wears a white top with a scoop neck and a pair of slim jeans. Her date doesn't deserve her. I don't know who he is, what he does, or a thing about him, but I don't need to. He doesn't fucking deserve this amazing humor-producing, big-hearted, glorious-chested, kitchen-talented woman. "You asked a ridiculous question, Chase."

Sternly, I say, "You're the one who wanted to tell me your last-known location."

"I'm just being cautious. Not paranoid."

I relent. "Sorry."

"But, seriously. I have a favor to ask." There's no toying in her tone.

"Of course. Ask me anything." *And I'll do it.*

Her voice is innocent, hopeful even as she asks, "Can I call you if anything comes up?"

"Like what?"

"I don't know," she says, fidgeting with a heart charm on her silver bracelet. "Just anything, I guess. I saw Henry once over the summer, and we had a nice time, then he had to leave town for an assignment. I don't know much about him, and usually my friend Lily, who runs the flower shop down the street from me, is my backup. But she's out with her boyfriend Rob tonight, so if anything happens, can you be my Bat-Signal?"

When she puts it like that, how can I harbor a ball of frustration over her dating? I might think she's a babe, but first and foremost she's my friend. One of my best friends. I stride across the hardwood floor, drape an arm around her, and pull her in close to reassure her.

Except . . . tactical error.

I draw a deep inhale of her hair. That ball of frustration doesn't unwind. It coils, because . . . he'll smell her tonight. He'll know her cherry scent.

My fists clench. My chest pinches. My jaw tightens.

But then, I'm just being territorial, I tell myself. I'm a lion protecting my pride.

This isn't personal. This isn't a man looking out for his woman. This is just elemental. It's basic male/female pack mentality, king-of-the-jungle shit. It's a guy looking out for a girl he cares about. My job is to be her wingman on alert. To keep her safe. "You know I will, Josie, baby," I say in her ear.

Baby?

What the fuck? I don't use terms of endearment. I don't utter sweet little nothings.

"Thank you," she says as we separate. "It's just this whole online dating thing is . . ." She draws a deep breath. "It's fraught with challenges. I went out with someone a few months ago, and, well, let's just say it didn't work out."

"Relationships have a way of doing that."

She nods and quirks up her lips. "But I'm glad to have you to lean on."

I tilt like the Tower of Pisa. "Lean on me."

She nudges her shoulder against mine, and my heart beats faster. Like, way speedier than the normal resting heart rate. That's odd. But I tell myself the quickened pace comes from a simpler place—from the human desire to be needed. The best gal I know needs me to be her reliable, steady guy. That's what I'll be for her. I won't be the dude who thinks about her chest, or her legs, or her intoxicating hair. Hell, I already know that kicking a friendship up a notch can fuck up all sorts of shit.

It can ruin everything.

Including the heart.

When Josie steps away from me, the beating in my chest returns to normal. I point at her. "For you, I make house calls. The doctor is always in."

She thanks me again, and I leave to meet my buddies at Joe's Sticks, a pool hall in the east Fifties. Max, Spencer, Nick, and Wyatt are at a table, racking up. Max claps me on the back when I arrive. "How's life on a sitcom working out for you?"

"Har, har, har."

He thrusts a beer at me. "Three's company yet?"

I take the bottle. "Except there's only two of us."

His dark eyes stare me down. "I can count. I can also speculate. And that little number—two—tells me it'll be even harder for you," he says, shaking his head as he hands me a pool cue. "You're on my team. And I can't wait to say I told you so."

"That's what I love about you. The endless well of support."

"Always," he says with a wink. He nods at the table. "You go first. I need my ringer."

I say hello to the other guys and then line up my shot. I'm good at pool. It's the focus. The concentration. The same skill set as sewing up a forehead. Yes, I have excellent hand-eye coordination, and it helps me kill it at the pool table. Max is a beast, too, so we're like the one-two Summers brothers' punch.

I line up and aim. I send the white ball straight into the purple ball, which races over the felt and rattles neatly into the corner pocket.

"Nice one," Wyatt says from the corner of the table. Earlier, he texted me that his wife, Natalie, would be busy tonight doing wedding prep with Spencer's wife, Charlotte. Yes, *wedding prep*. Wyatt and Natalie are already married, but they're getting married again. They tied the knot in Vegas a little while ago, but they're having a ceremony here in a few weeks for friends and family.

As I walk around the table, looking for the next shot, Wyatt says, "How's life with my little sister?"

"Great," I say. Because it is.

"What's she up to tonight?"

I pause for a second, unsure if I should say what she's doing. "She's out."

Spencer parks his hands around his mouth like a megaphone. "Code word for date."

Nick straightens his spine and arches a brow at Spencer. "Seriously? My sister does not date."

Spencer smacks his back. "Yup. Just like my sister didn't date," he says, giving him a sharp I-caught-you stare since Nick's engaged to Spencer's sister Harper.

Nick holds up his hands. "Fine, fine."

Spencer pokes Nick with the cue. "Get used to it, buddy. Get used to your sister dating. I had to get used to it with you, of all people."

I sink my shot, then miss the next one. When Nick takes his turn, Wyatt calls out to me, "Who's the lucky guy tonight, and when do we need to beat him up?"

I shrug. "Don't know."

He stares sharply at me. "You don't know?"

"Dude, I'm not her keeper."

"I know, shithead. But you need to look out for her." Wyatt points his beer bottle at me.

"Yeah, because men are pigs," Max says, weighing in.

We all hold up our beers at that statement.

Later, Wyatt pulls me aside. "Seriously, man. Look out for Josie. She dated some guy last spring who really hurt her."

Like a chemical reaction, that searing jealousy from earlier transforms into an entirely new substance—the wish to hurt this guy. "Who's this assfuck? The guy she's out with tonight? Henry?"

Wyatt shakes his head and blows out a long stream of air. "Not Henry. I don't have all the details. She told Natalie, but basically this guy she met online totally wooed her, and when they met in person it was clear all he wanted was . . ."

I clench my teeth. "Fuck, I hate douches."

"Yeah, me too."

"What happened?"

"He blew her off after he got what he wanted."

"Classic dick move."

"Classic," Wyatt agrees. "I swear if she had told me who he was I'd probably have killed him, and it's not even like he committed the worst dating sin ever. But he hurt my sister. Ergo . . ."

"You want to kill him," I supply.

"I hate people who hurt my sister. I need you to watch out for her. Just like I'd do for Mia if you needed me to." My sister

Mia's on the West Coast, working her butt off to build up her company, and she's doing great as far as I can tell from her regular texts and emails. "You're in Josie's space now, man. You're going to know better than anyone else what's going on. Be her fucking online dating profile decoder."

I hold up a fist for knocking. "Count on it."

This role now? This is what matters. It's a jungle out there, and if there's anything I can do to help Josie Hammer navigate her way through it, I will. I can sniff out a douchebag. I can protect her from the fuckers of the world.

When she calls me a little later, I've got my first assignment.

"Doctor Decoder at your service," I joke, stepping away from my buds.

"He's choking," Josie says. Loud music plays in the background, and she sounds rattled and on her way to panicked. I go into instant ER mode.

"What's going on?"

"My date. Henry. He's choking and can barely talk, and he's got an EpiPen in his hand, but he's struggling to use it. Do I just stab it in his thigh?"

Her voice is strained, understandably, jammed with the nerves I've heard countless times from others in her situation.

"Yes," I say, all-business as I march out of the noisy pool hall. I'll text Wyatt later and let him know where I went. "It's easy. Jab it in his thigh, click it, and I'll be there in five minutes."

"Stay on the phone with me," she says, her voice shaky.

"Absolutely." I hail a cab and zip over a few blocks to Bar Boisterous, keeping her calm the whole way as her date starts to breathe again.

Once inside, I quickly find Josie with a bearded hipster dude and take over for her. I help him out of the bar, and we take him to the nearest emergency room.

Even though it's a busy Saturday night, they see him stat, and it's not just because he has a personal escort with an MD. It's because Josie's date came *this* close to having one hell of a bad ending to his night.

The guy's allergic to peanuts, and there were trace amounts in the pesto sauce in the sandwich he ordered at Bar Boisterous.

Two hours later, we leave Henry safe and sound with the doctors and nurses. They'll take care of him now, and make sure he's doing fine.

The hospital doors close behind us, and I turn my attention once more to Josie.

CHAPTER TEN
From the pages of Josie's Recipe Book

Waffles with Strawberries
May Lead to Unexpected Moments

Ingredients

2 cups strawberries, quartered

2 eggs

2 cups flour

1½ cup milk

½ cup butter, melted

2 tablespoons white sugar

4 teaspoons baking powder

¼ teaspoon kosher salt

2 teaspoons vanilla extract

Directions

1. Preheat your waffle maker according to its instruction manual.

C'mon, you know you have the manual. This is the first time you're making waffles from scratch. Admit it.

2. While it is heating, prepare your batter. Add one cup of strawberries to your blender. Puree until smooth.

Don't get distracted by words in recipes like "smooth," which is how you picture Chase's chest.

3. Add the eggs, butter, milk, and vanilla extract to the strawberries, and blend until smooth. Add half the flour, sugar, salt, and baking powder, and do the same. Add the remaining flour mixture and blend until well mixed. Stir in the remaining strawberries.

Funny thing. Strawberries remind me of Chase's favorite dessert—the yummy strawberry shortcake cupcakes I make for the Sunshine Bakery. I should really make him some. I like the way his hazel eyes light up when he eats them, as if they're the best thing he's ever tasted.

4. When your waffle maker is preheated, spray with cooking spray and begin making your waffles. Pour the batter into one corner and smooth into the other corners with a spatula. Cook. Remove waffles from waffle maker and set aside. Repeat until all waffles are made. Or until you decide to go out for waffles at one of the many amazing establishments in Manhattan that make way tastier waffles than even a baker can make.

Bonus—no clean-up or storage of a ridiculously heavy object. Besides, having waffles with Chase is more proof of how well we fit as roomies, especially since I want to talk to him about that crazy date that just ended.

CHAPTER ELEVEN

Out on the street, Josie breathes a huge sigh of relief, then plants her hands on my shoulders. "I can't thank you enough."

A cab squeals by, on a hunt for a fare at the end of the block. I wave away her thank-you. "Don't even think twice about it. I barely did a thing."

She squeezes my shoulders harder, her eyes pinned on me. "No. You did everything."

"You're the one who worked the EpiPen. You hardly even needed me."

She shakes her head. "You're wrong. I totally needed you. Being able to call you, having you join me, taking him to the hospital . . . Chase," she says, taking a beat, "that was everything."

It wasn't everything, not even close, but I can't deny that my heart fucking races from the compliment. I wish I didn't like it so much.

She tilts her head. "I'm starving. Want to go to Wendy's Diner and order waffles? On me."

My growling stomach is the answer. "Waffles on you is my dream meal."

She nudges me and shoots me a smile as we walk along the sidewalk. "King of double entendres."

"And I wear the title with pride," I say, trying my best to think about waffles, not eating them off Josie. Though I bet that's the absolute best way to eat waffles.

Under the bright fluorescent lights at Wendy's Diner around the corner, curiosity gets the better of this cat. After the waitress brings water and coffee and takes our order, I stroke my chin, as if I've got a beard. "Beards. Glasses. Skinny jeans."

She frowns in confusion. "Is that your grocery list?"

"No. But is it yours? Would I have received an *aardvark* text warning me to stay away tonight? Are you into hipsters?" I nod in the general uptown direction of the hospital. I've never thought about who she might be into before. It hasn't been a big part of our lexicon. The fact is, I'm only vaguely aware of a few dates and boyfriends she's had in the past. I am well aware, though, that of all the things I might be, a hipster is absolutely not one of them.

I'm not sure why my muscles tense as I wait for her answer. Or why I hope she doesn't have a big thing for hipsters.

She laughs and takes a drink of her water. She shrugs happily. "I don't really have a type."

My shoulders relax. "You just like all dudes?"

She rolls her eyes. "No. Obviously I don't like everyone. But I don't have a physical type per se. Sure, handsome is nice, but it's not a prerequisite that he has tats or not, or a beard or not, or burly muscles or not, or red hair or not, as examples."

I drag a hand through my hair, unable to resist flirting with her, even now. "Light brown hair. That'd do the trick nicely, though?"

She stretches a hand across the Formica table and rubs my hair. "Yes, and warm hazel eyes, and a nice square jaw, and strong arms, and a flat belly," she says, letting go, and my eyes widen at the litany of compliments while my body enjoys the got-her-to-cop-a-feel moment.

"Perhaps you should write *my* PlentyOfFish profile." I pretend to tap on a keyboard. "Type: Ridiculously handsome, chiseled jaw, eyes that melt a woman, brilliant wit, and as a bonus, great in bed."

She laughs. "Well, now that you mentioned the bonus features . . ."

I point at myself. "Just being honest and laying out all the key features of this type of car."

"I appreciate your frankness about the vehicles on the lot, Chase," she says, deadpan. Then she adds, "And yes, if I do have a type, ideally he's smart, funny, kind to animals, and treats women well."

"Also, he should be able to handle peanuts, right? Incidentally, I happen to love them."

She laughs. "Peanut aficionado is optional. Walnut lover is better, though. If he loves pecans, then we're talking the real deal."

"So mixed nuts it is. Duly noted." I mime making a check mark.

"Plus, bonus points for not being a liar," she says, taking her time on that last one as a waitress strides by, balancing three plates of scrambled eggs and bacon.

I grab my coffee and take a thirsty gulp. When I set it down, I ask, "So what's the story there? Wyatt mentioned some guy you dated."

She sighs, looks at the table, then back up. "It's stupid."

I slide my hand across the table and rest it on top of hers. "It's not stupid."

She shakes her head. "It's just . . . you put yourself out there, and someone isn't who he seems. Do you know what I mean?"

Do I ever.

"Yes."

"And this guy, Damien, was like that. I met him on an online site, and we just really hit it off. We connected on everything. Same sense of humor, same love of books. He even liked Scrabble."

A rocket-fueled blast of jealousy rolls through me. That's *our* thing. I grit my teeth as she talks.

"We had the best time chatting online. We'd chat until the wee hours of the morning about anything and everything. He changed his status to *exploring a new relationship*. And we went out a couple of times. They were all these seemingly perfect, idyllic dates," she says, and I hate Damien already with a bone-deep loathing. "We went to a piano bar, and even when he heard me sing under my breath, he didn't make fun of me." She flashes a weary smile. "And you know what an awful singer I am."

"Just mouth the words," I whisper.

Her smile grows bigger. "He doesn't know about that. You're the only one privy to that horror story."

During one of our college breaks at her house, while the two of us were hanging out in the living room, stretched out on her parents' couch, her feet slung over my thighs, I'd asked her for her most embarrassing moment.

"Hands down. Second grade. Music class."

My ears perked. "Tell me."

"Each student had to sing 'Scotland's Burning' in front of the group, and when it was my turn, I walked into the middle of the circle, opened my mouth and sang, 'Scotland's burning, Scotland's burning, look out, look out.' And I was sure I sounded fine. Until the teacher covered her ears."

"Ouch."

"The real ouch was when the music teacher said, 'Just mouth the words, child. Just mouth the words.'"

"And that was the end of your Broadway dreams."

She imitated squashing a bug with her hand, and then she sang a line from the song. She was woefully off-key, and I joined in, committing equal musical crimes with my terrible voice.

"Don't tell my brothers."

"It's our secret," I'd said.

And it has been. Ever since.

"Anyway," she says, returning to the story of Damien. "The next time, he took me to a book signing. JoJo Moyes was in town, and he knew I loved her work so we went to An Open Book, where I met her and had her sign *Me Before You*."

My hatred for him intensifies. Josie loves that book. And I just know that somehow this douche nozzle used that information to take advantage of her. "You told me all about it last year. How torn up you were over the ending. How it made you think about so many things."

She nods, a small smile playing on her lips. "It did. I'm not saying I agree with the choices made, but that book just touched me," she says, patting her heart. Then she moves her hand to her head, tapping her temple. "And it made me think."

"I liked hearing your reaction when you wrote to me about it."

"And I liked sharing that with you," she says, then takes a beat. "And I told him, too. How it made me think. How it made me feel." She heaves a sigh. "So he took me to the signing. He was trying to be everything he thought I wanted, so he could get what *he* wanted."

She swallows, and yup, I know where this story is going. And it's not because Wyatt gave me the spoiler. It's etched in her eyes and colors her voice, and I wish I could erase any hurt she's ever been through. "A few more dates, a few more kisses, a few more times rolling out the Josie Hammer red carpet." She glances away momentarily, then she shakes her head and looks at me. "Then we slept together."

And even though I knew that was coming, I can't control the green-eyed monster that thrashes in my belly, fighting to break free.

I can, however, control what I do about it.

"And?" I ask, keeping my tone even.

"It was good," she says, matter-of-factly, and the creature rattles the bars, kicking and screaming. But I don't give in.

"And he didn't call the next day?"

A deep breath. A sheen over her eyes. "I waited. Stupidly." Her voice is feather-thin. "Like my phone was an extension of my hand. I even texted him the next evening. Like a foolish girl. 'Hey,'" she says, adopting a too-cheery tone. "'Hope you had a great day. I know I did. Thinking of you.'"

My stomach churns with anger. With righteous rage. "Did he ever write back?"

She nods. "Once. That night. He said, 'Day was great.'"

The dude couldn't even say *my* day was great.

"And is that all you ever heard from him?"

"Yes. He changed his status to *available and looking* the next morning. And I never heard from him again."

"He's one of the biggest wastes of space on the planet," I say as I squeeze her hand. "He doesn't deserve you, and he's a complete ass for leading you on. If he walked through the door right now, I'd . . ." I search the table, and grab an orange bottle. I brandish it like a weapon. "I'd douse his eyes with Tabasco."

She smiles. "But that'd be a waste of good Tabasco."

I grab the pepper shaker. "Line up a dozen pepper shakers outside the door, and lurk in the corner till he tripped on them, bonking his skull in the process."

Her smile turns to a full-blown grin. "Now you're tempting me."

I hold a finger in the air. "Wait. I've got it. Record myself singing 'Scotland's Burning' and hack his phone so it plays repeatedly, driving him insane with my horrible singing voice."

She laughs so loudly she snorts. It's fucking adorable and rewarding at the same time. "If we really want to torture him, we'd make it a duet," she says, her green eyes twinkling with the prospect of an epic prank.

I hold up my hand for a high five. She slaps my palm then weaves her fingers through mine. I squeeze back, then lightly drag my fingertips over the soft skin of her hand. Her eyes flicker with something else now, a different type of excitement, one I haven't seen from her before, but one I find I want more of.

The look vanishes too quickly when the waitress arrives.

"Waffles for two," she says in her thick Long Island accent, snapping her gum as she serves the plates.

We thank her, and when the waitress leaves, Josie picks up her fork. "Seriously, though, what can you do? Everyone gets Damiened sooner or later. It's not like something so terrible happened to me. It just hurt, but I'm over it. I wanted you to know, though, since you asked."

"Hey, don't discount it because it happens to others. A stomachache from the flu might not be as bad as appendicitis, but both can hurt."

She smiles. "That's true."

"I'm just sorry I wasn't here to kick his ass." I dig into my waffles. "Also, this needs to be said. But . . . Damien? Wasn't that kind of an omen? Get it? Because of the movie?"

She laughs. "I'm learning to read the signs. Clearly, I have a way to go. But now you're here, and I have a live-in translator."

"Twenty-four/seven dude-deciphering service," I say, then take a bite of a delicious square of waffle. "What about Henry? Will you see Mr. Peanut again?"

She shrugs. "I don't know. He was nice, but there was no spark."

I pump a virtual fist, and rein in a wild grin. "What does it take to get a second date with the inimitable Josie Hammer?" I ask as I slice another chunk of waffle. "Tell me. What is it that you're looking for in a man?"

The corner of her lips quirks up. "I want what every woman wants."

"What's that?"

She cocks her head. Gazes right into my eyes. Licks her lips. "The full package. I want the full package."

Chapter Twelve

When we return to the apartment, I grab her sleek silver laptop from the wooden coffee table. It's late on Saturday, but I don't care. "I'm off tomorrow and so are you. There are no excuses. Show me. Let's see who's got you swiping right or whatever you call it on your dating site."

I sink into our comfy couch, settling into one of the millions of pillows that have multiplied like bunnies thanks to Ms. Hammer's pillow-philia.

She grabs a hair tie from the table and loops her light brown strands into a knot on her head. A few pieces fall around her face, framing her cheeks with pink strands. Her lips are glossy, and it occurs to me she must have reapplied lipstick at some point. Maybe when I made a pit stop in the little boy's room at the diner. I'm sure I would have noticed her slicking some on. I would have watched, liking the way she looked when her lips formed an *O*. I linger too long on that letter and all its delicious possibilities. How she'd look when her mouth fell open in pleasure when she called out my—

Shake it off, buddy.

I remind myself of my special talent—separating feelings and thoughts. Because appreciating her lips doesn't mean I want to kiss them. And it doesn't mean I can't be her lookout.

"You really want to see the guys?" she asks, parking herself next to me and tucking her feet underneath her.

"Hell, yeah." I can't let her be Damiened again. I guarantee I would have been able to tell he was the kind of asshat who'd do that shit. No disrespect to Josie, but chicks can't always tell. I speak dude perfectly, and I'm going to translate for her to make sure she gets what she wants and deserves in life.

She flips open the screen, toggles over to her dating site, and clicks on a profile picture. The guy looks to be about forty, and he smiles like a realtor.

"This is Bob. Apparently, he messaged me tonight."

I rub my palms together. "All right. What does Bobby boy have to say?"

She opens the message on the site and reads aloud, "Hey there, Baker Girl. I like your pic. You're totes cute. We have a lot in common. I like books, too."

I stare her down, bring my hands to my armpits, and sway my shoulders back and forth like an ape. "Me like books. Books are good."

"At least he didn't start with asking me what kind of sex I like," she says, like that makes his opening line less Neanderthalic.

I shake my head. "Allow me to the do the honors." I swipe him closed for her. "What else have we got?"

She peers at the screen, pointing to a message from Fire-Trev. "How about Trevor? He's a firefighter."

I read the tagline on his profile. "Baby, can I light your fire?" I arch a brow. "Swiped."

She grabs my arm. "Is that any worse than you saying, 'the doctor is in'?"

"One, I'm not on an online dating site, so I wouldn't be saying that. And two, no. Which is why if I ever said that on an online dating site, you should throat-punch me."

Her lips twitch mischievously. "With a crème brûlée torch?"

"Consider it your throat-punching device of torture when I exceed the maximum acceptable level of douchery."

"There are actually acceptable levels?"

I shrug. "Look, you can't expunge douchiness completely. It's like a cockroach. It'll survive a nuclear explosion. It's a very tenacious quality in a man. I find it best to accept that there are levels of douchiness one can live with, usually manifesting as cockiness, confidence, or bravado." I narrow my eyes. "You gonna be okay with that harsh reality?"

She nods, intense as a soldier. "Those seem an allowable standard."

I tip my chin to the screen and inch closer to her. "What else have we got?"

Grabbing a cranberry red pillow between us, she tosses it on the back of the couch. Interesting. She's made more room. She pats the vacated spot, so I move closer as she clicks on a new message. The profile pic is a too-suave image of a dark-haired man in a sharp suit. "That screams I-got-my-profile-pic-from-a-stock-photo-site."

"Probably. Let's see what he says."

The message fills the screen as she reads, "I'm going to ask you a series of questions. Here's the first. Would you ever date a guy who likes to wear your panties?"

I snap my gaze to her. "Is this shit for real?"

She laughs. "Yes. Sadly, it is."

"This is ridiculous," I sneer. I'm this close to swiping when an evil idea lands in my brain. "Can I reply?"

"What are you going to say?"

"Do you trust me?"

The look in her eyes says *duh*. "Yes. But . . ."

I crack my knuckles. "Allow me to take the wheel."

She grabs my arm. "You're not going to write anything crazy, are you?"

"Nothing that won't amuse you." I hover my fingers above the keys then type, speaking the words out loud: "Sure, but only if he wears my panties on his head. To work."

She clasps her hand over her mouth, laughing. I take that as a sign to keep this shit up.

The next question from Captain Suave is: "What is the most exciting type of intimate video for you to watch?"

Hell if I'm not eager to know what gets her off, but that's not the point. I write back to the suit dude: "The kind your mother stars in."

Josie laughs loudly, then I read his next question. "How often do you come every week?"

I turn to her, and even though I'm dying for her weekly orgasm count more than Suave in a Suit can know, now isn't the time. I reply with, "Great question. I'd love to answer it, but maybe we could start the interview with some simpler questions. The last book you read, what kind of cereal you like, do you wear socks?"

The guy must have just come online and seen her newest message first, because his reply to that one is swift.

"*Catcher in the Rye*. I don't like cereal. Tube socks."

I slam the machine closed and give her a pointed look. "*Catcher in the Rye* is high school required reading, and if that's the last book he read, God help us. Plus, tube socks are a deal breaker. And you can't date someone who doesn't like cereal. There's no excuse for that."

She crosses her heart. "I solemnly swear to uphold the love of cereal." She sets the laptop on the table. "Okay, so we've clearly established tonight that there are lots of fish to wade through, that the love of certain breakfast foods is inviolate, and that a woman needs to allow for a teeny amount of douchery in her men. Correct?"

I nod sharply. "You are correct."

"I'm learning," she says, then tucks a strand of pink-streaked hair behind her ear, her silver bracelet sliding down her arm. "But what about you?"

I frown in confusion. "What about me?"

"Why are you so against online dating? Is it because of Adele? What happened with her, exactly? I've never known why it ended."

I sigh. *Adele.* Things with her ended two years ago. Before Africa.

With her sharp wit and brilliant mind, Adele and I hit it off instantly as residents together, becoming fast friends. Then we became more. She was smart, outgoing, and had the best bedside manner. And by bedside manner, I do mean bedside manner.

Redheaded and leggy and wildly sexual, Adele had seemed like the perfect woman for me. She also liked to experiment.

"Let's just say the leasing agent wasn't the first woman to invite me to a threesome," I tell Josie.

She stares at me expectantly and makes a quick, rolling gesture with her hand as if to say *tell me, tell me.*

"She thought one of the nurses, a brunette named Simone, was quite hot, and she asked me if I'd consider a threesome.

Honestly, that wasn't my thing. I'm a one-woman kind of guy."

"No interest in a threesome at all?"

I shake my head. "Nope. Don't want it. Don't need it. Not my cup of tea or brandy or Jack Daniels. But she wanted to. It was her fantasy, and I was crazy about her. I wanted to give it to her because it was what she wanted."

Josie leans closer. "Was that hard, servicing two women at the same time?"

I scoff. "Nope. Because I didn't."

"Didn't do it?"

"Didn't take care of them both. They took care of each other. I was kind of the third wheel."

She furrows her brow. "That's . . . weird?"

I shrug. "A little, maybe."

"So you split up because of a weird threesome?"

I shake my head. "No. I don't care about one weird sexual encounter. I mean, we're all bound to have that, right?"

"Sure."

"What bothered me was that Adele, my best friend at the time, went on to spend the next several months having an emotional affair with Simone."

Josie's jaw drops.

"I don't know if it was more or less devastating than if she'd been physically cheating, too. All I know is when she broke up with me, she told me she was in love with Simone and had been *emotionally involved* with her since the threesome."

Her jaw snaps shut, as she whispers, "That is rough."

"Yeah, and it wasn't a secret around the hospital. Everyone knows each other's business. And some of the docs said, 'Don't let it bother you—you don't have a pussy, so you never stood a chance.'" That was the way a few of my buds had tried to downplay the split. "Fine, she likes women, and she figured it out with me. I'm man enough not to freak out and think I turned her gay. That's not the issue. But just because I didn't have the right equipment," I say, my eyes straying to my crotch, "didn't make the breakup hurt less."

Josie runs a hand down my arm. "It's not about the equipment. It's not about whether you stood a chance with her. It's about this. Your heart," she says, placing her palm on my chest. Her touch feels good, and all my instincts tell me to grab her hand and hold it tight to me. Because I like the way it feels when her hands are on me.

Big shock.

"Exactly. But there was this sense among our colleagues that it should only have hurt if she screwed someone who had a dick. Who cares? That's not the issue. The issue is we were friends, then we were together, and then she fell in love with someone else and was involved with that person while she was with me. It doesn't hurt any less simply because I could never"—I sketch air quotes—"compete. And what sucked the most was that I missed her in my life."

That's how I learned the hard way that taking friendships to another level only results in heartache.

"I'd miss you if you weren't in my life," Josie says softly.

My muscles tighten with that fresh reminder to keep all thoughts of Josie on *this* level—the friendship one.

Her eyes roam over me, settling on my shoulders. "You're so tense," she says softly, then shifts her body, moving behind me, nudging me away from the back of the couch. And before I know it, she's rubbing my shoulders.

It's totally unexpected to have Josie's hands on me. She's comforting me, even though I'm not hurt anymore. But still, she seems to want to, and holy hell, is she ever talented at this. She digs her fingers into my shoulders, and it feels really fucking good. So good I groan.

"Jesus, Josie. You have great hands."

"It comes from kneading dough," she says, and I laugh then lean back into her, resting against her chest as she rubs my shoulders. I'm a hedonist, I'm a cat, I'm a complete pleasure-taker right now. But Josie's hands are magic, and I have no choice but to succumb to them.

"Your shoulders are tight, sweetie," she says, her breath soft, tickling my neck.

Sweetie. Baby.

We've both used terms of endearment for each other tonight. What the hell is that about?

But when her thumbs dig into my muscles, I don't think anymore. I shut off my mind and give in to the extraordinary feeling of her hands on me. I moan and murmur, "Feels so good."

I can sense her shifting behind me. Moving her face closer. Her lips are near my hair. "Good. Let me make you feel better."

She makes me feel worlds better, even though I didn't really feel bad. But I feel spectacular as she works my shoulders. It's better than good. It's good everywhere, including below the Mason–Dixon line, where there's a huge statue pointing out how much better than good this is.

It's arousing.

It's a turn-on.

With my eyes closed and her hands massaging me, my mind floats away, picturing her sliding her hands down my chest, reaching for the bottom of my T-shirt, tugging it over my head.

My dick hardens more as I imagine her return route—those soft, strong hands playing across my abs, traveling up my stomach to my pecs, exploring me.

I let out a breath. It sounds like a turned-on groan. Because I don't stop the fantasy there. As she touches me, I imagine her hands gliding into my hair, her lips brushing across my neck, her scent everywhere.

And then I see myself doing the next logical thing.

The only thing.

Flipping around, sliding her under me, pinning her wrists above her head.

And fucking her.

Even though I'm only her friend, even though I'm keeping it on the level, all signs in my head and body point to a different agenda.

Josie Hammer turns me on, and that's a big fucking problem.

CHAPTER THIRTEEN

A few days later, I find a clear plastic bag from her bakery on the coffee table. There's an assortment of mixed nuts inside —pecans, walnuts, and peanuts, too. Dangling from a yellow ribbon is a notecard.

Thanks again for coming to the rescue this past weekend. What would I do without a nut lover like you?

I smile and save the card, then pop some nuts in my mouth on the way to work.

* * *

The next few weeks at the hospital pass in a blur of gunshot wounds, chest pain, shower falls, drug overdoses, boiling water spills, and an apple where the sun doesn't shine.

The man who became intimately acquainted with the fruit told me he fell on a basket of Granny Smiths while sweeping the floors. "I like to keep them around, easily accessible. Apples are good for you," he'd said, while explaining away his . . . predicament.

In his case, the apple a day didn't keep the doctor away.

There was also an afternoon shift when the paramedics rushed in an incredibly polite British man who had collided with a wooden post at a construction site. "I seem to have acquired a splinter," he'd said, of the half-foot-long piece of wood in his ribs.

Ouch.

Today, we encountered a surprise baby.

When I return home, I tell Josie the story as she slides a lasagna dish out of the oven to check on it. I lean against the doorframe of the tiny kitchen, savoring the aroma of her cooking. "The girl was eighteen. She came in complaining of food poisoning. When we informed her she was pregnant and dilated to ten centimeters, she told us she was going to sue us for defamation of character."

"Well, naturally. Being told you're pregnant by a doctor is complete and absolute grounds for a courtroom trial, I'm sure," she says as she closes the oven door. "Five more minutes for this."

"Then she started pushing, and when the baby came out, her first words were, 'It's not mine. It needs to go back to its mama. Send it back to its real mom.'"

Josie frowns. "Awww. Poor baby."

I nod. "Yup."

She tilts her head. "Do you think she just didn't want to be pregnant and was trying to deny it, or was she mentally unstable?"

"Hard to say. The girl's not the first one to come into the ER saying she didn't know she was pregnant."

"But if she doesn't want the kid, what happens to the baby?"

I shrug as I grab a grape from a glass bowl on the counter and pop it into my mouth. "Don't know. That's for the hospital social worker to figure out."

"I wish there was something we could do for the baby," she says softly.

"It's going to be fine. The baby is healthy," I say, since that's really all I know.

Worry is etched onto her features as her brow furrows. "But how do you know it's going to be fine?"

Her question gives me pause. Makes me think. "I don't entirely know, but I *trust* that the appropriate people will help both of them."

She sighs heavily and shakes her head. "But for a second, just think about what happens next. What is life going to be like for either one of them?"

I shrug, half wishing I could give her the answer she wants, and half wishing she'd stop asking. I don't always like to contemplate what happens next to my patients. *Next* isn't always pretty. *Next* isn't always good. I do all I can do in the exam room. I can't start marinating on the pieces of everyone's life that I have zero control over.

She peers at the clock on the stove. "I can't help it. I feel bad for both of them."

I hold up my hands in surrender. "She's going to be fine."

She shoots me a skeptical stare. "Who? The baby? The mother?"

I stare at her back. "Both, I presume."

Her voice escalates in a mix of sadness and irritation. "You can't just presume that."

I nod. "Yes. I can. It's part of the job."

She shakes her head and knits her brow. "I don't get it. How can you separate everything so easily? How can you say she'll be fine when you don't actually know?"

I take a breath and call upon my best cool demeanor. Josie's getting emotional. She's becoming attached to patients that aren't even hers. I need to talk down the Florence Nightingale in her. "Hey," I say calmly, setting a hand on her arm. "We have people at the hospital who can help. We have a great social worker. We'll do everything we can. The only way I could assist her medically was to focus on the physical. Now there are others who will help her, okay?"

She draws a huge breath, like she's gulping up oxygen after being deprived. When she nods as if she's settled, I'm ready to write this off as done, but then she slides past me. "Excuse me," she mumbles, her voice hitching, then she's off and seconds later the bathroom door slams closed.

"Fuck," I mutter.

And I wait. And I wait. And I wait.

When the timer beeps on the oven, I half figure that Josie's internal baker clock will ding and summon her from the bathroom. But after sixty seconds, she's still MIA, so I grab a potholder, pull out the lasagna, and set it on a cooling rack. Staring at it for a minute, I decide on a game plan. I don't know what Josie's upset about, but I can only fix what I can fix.

The rest of dinner.

I hunt around for a bottle of wine, grab a merlot, and un-screw the cork. When I find two glasses, I set them on the coffee table in the living room that doubles as our dining room table. I add cloth napkins—the only kind we use, since Josie's taught me that paper ones are wasteful to the environment. When I return to the kitchen, I grab two sunshine-yellow plates, then a spatula. I serve a chunk of lasagna for her, then one for me.

As I set the plates on the table along with forks, she rounds the corner, a wad of tissue in her hands. "I'm so sorry," she says, her voice thin with tears. Her expression is soft now and apologetic. "I didn't mean to push so hard about a patient of yours."

"Don't think twice about it. But . . . are you okay?" I step closer to her.

"It's not you. I just . . ." She swipes at her cheeks with the tissues. "I just had a long day, and we ran out of seven-layer bars earlier than we'd advertised for the Tuesday special, and this customer came in and threw a complete fit that we were out, and said she was going to"—she stops to adopt a bitchy voice—"'rip us a new one' on Yelp. And I know it's a little thing in the scheme of all the big things, but I've worked so hard to build a good business after I took over for my mom, and sometimes all it takes is one bad review to shred you. So I've been waiting all day for the other shoe to drop, and on top of that my friend Lily's boyfriend is acting like a total dick, and I feel bad for her because she still likes him, but he's so not worth her time and I want her to realize it. And so I was making lasagna to try to get my mind off it all." Her words are tumbling out like she's in a confessional. "And then you come home, and you're so good at separating everything, and I just can't do that. I'm terrible at that." Another tear slips down her cheek.

I take a tissue and wipe it away. "You don't have to deal with things the way I deal with things. You're you, and you should deal with them as you need to."

She takes a deep breath and nods. "I wish I could just shut things off. Like you can."

"It's a blessing and a curse," I joke.

"It's a gift," she says emphatically.

"Well, look. I have to separate myself to some degree. I can't react to things the way a patient would, because if I did then I wouldn't be very good at taking care of them, right?"

She nods as I wrap an arm around her and guide her to the couch.

"I'm sorry I gave you a hard time," she whispers.

I shake my head. "Ha. That was hardly a hard time. And if you do decide to give me a hard time, I can handle it." I puff out my chest and hit it. "Steel, baby. I'm steel. I can take it."

She smiles, a rueful little grin.

"But look. Don't get frustrated that emotions spill over for you. It's who you are, and it's part of what makes you . . ."—I pause, looking for the right words—"one of the most amazing people I know."

She swats my shoulder. "Oh stop."

"Hey, you are," I say. Then I take a beat and quirk up my lips. "Honestly, though, I thought you were just having your period."

"You ass," she says.

"I totally am an ass. But this ass served dinner." I gesture to the meal. "Dine with me?"

"Why, I thought you'd never ask."

As we dig into the lasagna, my belly thanks her. I point with my fork to the plate. "This is the best thing I've ever tasted."

"You say that about everything I make."

"And I mean it about everything you make."

"Thank you," she says with a smile. "Oh, and in case you were wondering, my period was last week, and you didn't even notice."

"Damn, you're stealthy in the hormonal reaction department."

She nudges her shoulder into mine. "Sorry again. Do you forgive me?"

I meet her eyes, and for a second I'm tempted to run my hand through her hair, to brush my lips to hers, to kiss her softly to reassure her that we're all good.

Then I snap out of it.

Even so, I wish I could tell her the truth. That it's getting harder for me to pull off this trick. That she challenges my ability to compartmentalize like no one and nothing ever has. All my instincts tell me to kiss her, to touch her, to take her to bed.

But man can't let instincts rule him.

Mind over man, I remind myself.

The good news is when she checks Yelp again that night, her bakery still has a sterling average. I tell her the woman was all talk. When she kisses me good night—on the cheek—I clench my fists as a reminder to keep it all in check. As she turns on her heel and walks into her bedroom, my eyes don't stray from her, and that's the problem. It's become all too clear that these separate drawers are getting messier every day.

I'm not sure how to keep them closed.

But I vow to try.

CHAPTER FOURTEEN

Over the next few days, I recommit to my mission. My focus is on building and sustaining the friendship wing of the house of Josie and Chase, not the lust corridor.

Mostly, I succeed. I monitor Yelp and gleefully report that the troll never trolled. I pick up the tissues she likes when she runs low. And I offer my taste buds to be the guinea pig for her grapefruit macaron. She was right—it's amazing.

But all it takes is one moment for me to relapse.

She's in her bedroom, and the hallway is steamy, since she takes showers the temperature of the surface of Mercury. It's sauna level as I head into the bathroom to brush my teeth before I leave for an early morning bike ride with Max.

When I finish, she calls out to me, "Hey, Chase, are you still in the bathroom? I forgot to put my body lotion on while I was in there."

"Which kind? I'll bring it to you."

"The black cherry one," she shouts. "Top shelf on the wooden cabinet."

Oh, that's another thing about living with a woman. They commandeer all available bathroom real estate. My sister, Mia, was like this, too, so I learned as a teenager how to survive with very little space. Here with Josie, I've managed to claim squatter's rights to a corner of the medicine chest where my deodorant and shaving cream live. The rest? She's encroached on all of it.

I grab the lotion, putting my cherry-scented fantasy of dragging my tongue between the heavenly valley of her breasts into a chaste drawer, the same one where I keep thoughts of kittens, puppies, and baby ducks. Proximity to the cuteness will rub off and turn the naughty to wholesome, right?

Her bedroom door is open, but I knock anyway. "Come in," she says, and when I open the door all the way, I'm not ready to take this test. No fucking way can I pass it.

"Did you need a towel to go with the dishtowel you're using?" I ask, because humor production is the only way I can deal with the fact that she has the world's tiniest towel cinched around her tits.

I'm not strong enough. I'm going to wave the white flag any second.

"Oh," she says, glancing down as she tugs upward on the material. "Laundry day. The only towel left was this one. I think it might be a hand towel."

"Safe bet," I say, as she tries to adjust the blue material covering her prized possessions and hitting her upper thigh on the other end. As she does, she kills all my good work of the last few days because she winds up revealing even more of that perfect, creamy flesh. The swell of her breasts is unveiled. My mouth waters. I drool. I foam. I fall to the floor in a heap of nothing but hormones and testosterone unleashed. Scientists for years will study me as an example of death by hotness overexposure.

She stares at me with her palm out.

I blink, somehow reconnecting my mouth to the last few remaining brain cells that haven't been obliterated. "Yeah. What?" I shake my head. "Did you say something?"

She laughs. "The lotion. May I have it?"

"Oh right," I say, staring at my hand like I just discovered it's attached to my body. Huh. I'm not actually dead. I didn't fall to the ground. I survived the overdose, and I'm alive and gawking. I hand the bottle to her. "Here you go."

With every ounce of resolve in me, I leave, grab my bike from the basement, and ride downtown to meet Max. Time with my brother is the best boner killer in the world.

Just to be safe, I add my sister to the mix when the ride ends, calling Mia as I lock up my bicycle in the basement at my building.

"Have you saved the world yet?" I ask when she answers.

My sister has a great laugh, warm and inviting. Goes perfectly with her dry sense of humor. "Just some more bunnies," she says.

Mia's company specializes in cruelty-free makeup and beauty products, and it's the culmination of her heart's desire since she was a kid – to save all the animals.

We catch up briefly then she has to leave to head to work.

The call with her does the trick, though, and keeps my mind off Josie's body.

But only for a few days.

On Friday night, Josie strolls through the living room, her heels clicking on the floor. I look up from the book I'm reading on my phone.

Tonight she wears a dress. A dark pink one that looks . . . wow. Just wow. Just utterly smoking hot. It hugs her hips and snuggles her breasts and shows off her strong, soccer-toned legs.

I blink a few times. Maybe ten. Maybe one hundred.

"Who's the lucky guy?" I ask in my best just-your-guy-friend-looking-out-for-you voice.

"I have a date with Paul tonight. He's the software project manager you picked out from the site. The only one you thought sounded normal, remember?"

"The rare find who used proper grammar and possessed the ability to ask questions about something other than lingerie and blow jobs," I say, since I figured eventually I had to give the okay to one of them, and he was the safest bet. "You're awfully fancy, though."

She shrugs as if it's no big deal. "I had the dress and haven't had the chance to wear it yet. I thought it'd be fun. I don't get to dress up for work."

Inside, I'm thinking she could dress up for me, like when we go to Bed Bath & Beyond, or grocery shopping, or even to pick up toilet paper. Maybe that's selfish, but so it goes.

"Well, he is a lucky son-of-a-bitch to see you in that dress."

She fiddles with a necklace. "I can't get this clasp. Can you help? My fingers are still slippery from putting on lotion."

I stand, brush my hands over my jeans, and step closer to her. She gathers up her hair, lifting it against the back of her head, exposing her neck. My throat goes dry. My skin prickles with desire. Her long, lovely neck looks spectacular. Prime real estate for kissing.

But I can't go there, so I take hold of the ends of the necklace, and though I toy with the idea of taking longer than necessary, I opt for being a gentleman. I close the keyhole quickly. As much as I might want to linger here all night, I can't give myself away.

"There," I say, and as she lowers her hair, I hope to hell Paul won't be the one unhooking that clasp tonight. As soon as that awful notion touches down, I ball my hands into fists, and I try to keep this jealousy at bay.

I hope she hates the guy. Because there's no way any man could be with her tonight and do anything but fall head over heels.

I leave shortly after she does. Lest I stay home like a date-less schmuck on a Friday night, I asked out a blond radiologist named Trish who likes to play fantasy baseball. I'm a big Yankees fan myself, so that gives us great conversation beyond the shop talk. At a sports bar nearby, we nurse beers and watch a game on the big screen, debating the best pitchers in baseball history. It's fine as far as dates go, but when it's time for that inevitable will we/won't we moment, I don't feel it, so I say good-bye to her.

As I wander through the streets of Murray Hill, listening to an audiobook about physics in everyday life while sidestepping the already inebriated packs of New Yorkers, I find that I'm looking forward to talking to Josie, way more than I'd wanted to go on a date, and hoping too that Paul was a bust.

When I open the door, the scent of seven-layer bars greets me. That must mean her date ended early, too. Which means I'm a happy camper.

I turn into the kitchen. She pulls a tray from the oven and smiles. She still wears the date outfit, but the heels are gone. She's adorable in her fancy dress and bare feet.

"Date ended early?"

She nods. "When he invited me to see his gerbil, I thought it was time to go."

"That doesn't entice you?"

She shakes her head. "Had he said ferret, perhaps. Alas, with gerbil I'm a firm no."

"Was it in his pants or a cage?"

"We didn't get far enough to find out. I said thanks, I need to water the plants, and I got the hell out of Dodge."

I curl up the side of my mouth. "Guess that explains why Trish didn't invite me home, either. I tried the hamster line on her."

She smacks me with a panda potholder. "I suppose I should have known better, though. Earlier in the date, he made a ton of masturbation comments."

I lean against the kitchen counter. "And that concerns you, since you never do that, right?"

As she slides the spatula under the dessert, she gives me a side-eye stare. "Exactly, Chase. I never rub one out. Never." She waves a hand over her crotch. "Total hands-free zone."

I take her comment seriously. "Fine. You use toys. I get it. What kind?" I ask, because I can't help myself.

She rolls her eyes. "Not telling you."

I harrumph and grab for a bar from the pan. She swats me with the spatula.

"Ouch," I say, yanking back my hand.

"That didn't hurt. And you should know better than to steal my dessert before it's ready."

"You should know better than to hit my hands." I hold both up in the air.

With a quickness I don't see coming, she whacks me again with her utensil. This time on the other hand.

"That's it." I charge her, tickling her waist. "Tell me what toys and I'll stop."

She cracks up and flails her arms, knocking me with elbows and hands and the spatula, too, until I give in to her cries for mercy.

I stare at her in our tiny sliver of a kitchen. "Waiting."

"You really want to know?"

I nod eagerly. I'm playing with fire, but I can't resist. The desire to know outweighs all else.

She works the spatula under the bars again, shaking her head. "I can't believe we're having this conversation."

I hold out my hands. "C'mon. We talk about all sorts of stuff." Then, an idea strikes me. I open the kitchen cupboard, grab a bottle of Patron, and hold it up. "This will help all that shyness."

She stares at me with narrowed eyes. "I'm not shy at all."

I grab two shot glasses and pour. "Better safe than sorry, Miss Not Shy At All."

I hand her one, and she takes it. Then I raise my glass, and the drink goes down the hatch with a burn. She follows suit, swallowing it quickly, then sets her glass down. I do the same.

I rub my palms together. "Toy confessional time. What have you got?"

She arches an eyebrow. "Really? You really want to know?"

I narrow my eyes. "What part of your roommate being a dirty bastard do you not understand? Obviously, I want to know. I'm a guy. This is like Christmas morning. But if this helps . . ."

I pour two more shots then slide her glass over to her. Once more, we down them.

She draws a deep breath. "Since you asked . . . I have a few toys. A little silver bullet. A bigger dolphin. And I have a waterproof finger vibrator."

And the temperature in me shoots through the roof. I tug at the neck of my shirt. "For the shower?" I croak out.

"Seeing as we don't have a bathtub, yes, it would have to be for the shower."

"You masturbate in the shower?" I ask, and the visual is so fucking clear in my mind—Josie under a hot stream of water that slopes off her breasts, a finger vibrator working between her thighs.

She nods as she slides the bars onto a cooling rack. Just then I remember she promised me seven-layer bars when she freaked out the other night. And she delivered. Fuck, I think she might be perfect, what with her desserts and her shower hobby.

"Why do you ask?" she asks in a hyper-innocent voice. Then she clasps her fingers over her mouth. "Are you busy spanking the monkey in your bed while I'm sleeping?"

I point my thumb at myself. "Shower here, too, baby."

She arches an eyebrow. "I guess the shower's like a good priest. It keeps both our secrets." She gestures to the bars. "As soon as they cool off you can have one. Now, tell me, do you clean the shower when you're done?" She winks, grabs the tequila and the shot glasses, and heads to the couch.

I follow, like the dog that I am. Tongue hanging and panting, just waiting for a crumb to fall.

"I'm the neat one, remember?" I pat the back of the couch. "But I bet you don't only do-it-yourself in the shower. You probably did it on this couch before I moved in. This is a diddle couch, right? Just admit it."

"Well . . ." She twirls a strand of hair in her fingers, and takes her time doling out her answer. "I can't exactly watch porn in the shower."

I groan at her admission. The images whip fast and furious in my brain. "This is where you watch porn and get off?"

She laughs and grabs the bottle, pouring another round. She thrusts a glass at me, and this time we clink. She wiggles her eyebrows. "Yes, I've been known to watch porn from time to time."

Bringing the glass to her lips, she knocks it back. I match her shot for shot, and the liquor must be loosening both our tongues. We've always been pretty open, but this conversation is slip-sliding quite nicely in a whole new direction.

"Just from time to time?" I ask.

She shrugs naughtily, a little I've-got-a-secret look in her eyes.

"It's okay. Tell the doctor. Masturbation is normal. Don't be ashamed." I wrap her in a huge hug, as if I'm comforting her. Not because I'm trying to touch her. When we separate, I clear my throat. "So, seriously. What kind of intimate videos do you like?" I ask, adopting an interviewer's tone, as if I'm the dude on the site who asked that question.

Only, it was inappropriate from him. From me, the question is thoroughly acceptable, since it's all in the name of scientific research.

"You want to know?" she asks, her eyes wide as she holds my gaze.

God yes. So much. I'm dying to know what turns you on. "Of course I want to know what floats Josie's boat on the diddle couch." She tosses a pillow at me. I catch it. "Fine. Pleasure den. Can we call it your Pleasure Den of Personal Delights?"

"Only if I can call the shower your Whack Zone."

I let my jaw fall open in a shocked expression. "Fine, call it the Whack Zone. Just answer the question."

"Okay," she says, taking a breath and squaring her shoulders. "I like male-male porn."

I'm taken aback for a moment. "You do?"

"I do," she says with a nod, owning it. "Does that bother you? You seem surprised."

"I was surprised. But it doesn't bother me. To each her own."

"Your turn," she says, lifting her chin. "What do you like?"

The answer is easy. "I like videos of girls getting themselves off."

Her eyes widen, and I see a hint of desire in them. "Yeah?"

I nod.

"Why?" she asks, her voice soft but eager. Curiosity drips from her tone.

I shift, as if that'll relieve the pressure in my jeans. But it doesn't. My dick is trying to hit a new record for hardness right now, as if it's competing in the Erection Olympics. But I can't fault my dick. It's impossible to be anything but turned on during this conversation.

The tequila is helping my Honest Abe attitude this evening. Or maybe just living in close proximity to her is. For some reason, I don't feel like holding back tonight. "Because . . . there's something about the image of a woman all alone, so turned on she needs to take care of the business herself. No one else has to do a thing for her. She's just wildly aroused from her mind, her imagination. She closes her eyes. Her hand drifts down. She creates a fantasy in her head."

Josie draws a sharp breath. "That is hot," she whispers, and her voice sounds different. Aroused.

I stretch my arm across the back of the couch and paint with more words, loving this whole new direction of tonight's conversation. "I love seeing how wet she gets. Before she even takes off her panties. That really fucking turns me on."

I meet her eyes, and the green irises shine with unmistakable desire. I'm not hiding mine, either. Whether it's us momentarily lusting for each other, or just getting aroused by the conversation, I don't know. I don't care, either. I can't separate anything right now. I'm hard, and I bet she's wet.

"It's fun being wet," she says in a husky, smoky tone that seeps into my bones like a shot of pure, liquid lust. "I can see why you'd like watching that."

"And then it turns me the fuck on to watch a gorgeous woman spread her legs, touch herself, and then make herself come."

She blinks, then blows out a long stream of air and waves her hand in front of her face. "Wow. Those seven-layer bars baked on high in the oven. It is hot in here."

I tap her arm. Her breath hitches. "Your turn. Why do you like guy on guy?"

Her answer comes swiftly. "Because I like guys."

"Yeah?" I ask, remembering her comment about types. "But why that kind specifically?"

She brushes a strand of hair behind her ear and draws a deep breath. Maybe she's seeking courage, or maybe the liquid has already given it to her, because her answer is bold and hot. "I like what makes men *men*, and seeing two of them together turns me on even more. Look, I'm totally hetero. But that's why I like it," she says, and she reaches out a hand to my hair. "I like everything that makes a man a man. The hair."

She drags her hand through mine, and my eyes float closed. I savor her touch and the way desire shoots through my body from that simple act of her touching my hair.

"I like a masculine jawline," she says. She drags her thumb across mine, and lust curls like hot flames inside me.

I open my eyes and swallow harshly. I don't say a word. I don't have to. She's crafting a soliloquy to the male form, and I'm her muse right now. "I love stubble," she continues as she touches my face, demonstrating all her likes. Then her hand drifts to my arm. "And strong arms and muscles."

Her hand darts to my belly. Her eyes twinkle with mischief. She drops her voice to a sexy whisper. "I love a little happy trail, too."

And the fire goes wild. It torches my blood. It fucking consumes me. I'm not sure I'll ever cool off.

"That's why I like watching two guys," she finishes, as if she's summing up an answer to an exam question. "Men just turn me on. But I don't want to be in a threesome."

"What do you want?"

She juts up her shoulder. "One guy who wants me the way I want him."

Fuck this roommate situation. Fuck New York City housing. Fuck the horrors of finding four walls. I want to be that guy so badly.

"You should be worshipped. You deserve it," I say, my voice thick with lust I can't hide. "You're perfect."

Her lips part, and soft words fall from them. "So are you."

Here we are on the diddle couch, talking about what turns us on. I don't know how I ever thought I could cordon off sex from friendship and lust from emotion, but with Josie staring at me with heat in her green eyes, I have to exercise every ounce of my self-control.

Fortunately, she stands up and saves me from me. She smacks her forehead. "Totally forgot. I need to wash my hair." She nods. "I think I got some seven-layer bar in it."

"Yeah. You should wash the seven layers from your hair."

She turns the corner and heads to the bathroom.

This time I know she's not retreating. She's not crying. She's not sad. She's turned on.

Chapter Fifteen

A minute later, the water cranks on, the beat of the shower stream pounding against the tile. I close my eyes, my breath already coming hard, and I picture her naked. In my fantasy, I stand there, watching her. Her hands slide over her full breasts then slip between her legs. She doesn't even need her toy right now, she's so worked up.

And so the fuck am I. My dick is going to punish me if I don't deal with these epic levels of arousal right now.

Fuck it.

I can't stand this anymore. I've got to do something about this roommate situation. She's safely in the shower, and I'm safely in the living room. I unzip my jeans, slide my hand into my boxers and take my cock in my fist.

As the shower becomes my soundtrack, I stroke my dick, long, lingering strokes from the base to the tip. I run my other hand over my balls, which feel so fucking heavy. With lust for her. With absolutely inappropriate desire for my roommate, my good friend, my best friend's sister.

But what's a man to do?

Mere feet away from me, the woman of my dirty dreams is naked and playing with herself. That's my greatest fantasy. Josie is so turned on right now, she had to take care of business. God help me. I have no choice.

"Fuck," I mutter, because her pussy must be so slick and wet right now. So goddamn slippery.

I grip harder, sliding a bead of liquid over the head of my dick then down the shaft. It eases my solo flight. There's no time for buildup. No time to let this one last. I've got one mission and I'm on a fast track, headed for some much-needed relief.

She's probably nearly there herself, leaning against the shower wall under the stream, that lucky fucking water sliding all over her body.

With that glorious vision in my mind, I sink deeper into the couch and stroke. Longer, faster, rougher strokes. My fist curls tighter as I grip my dick and imagine the scene nearby. Her fingers fly. She doesn't take her time at all. She grabs her finger vibe, slides it on, and rubs her throbbing clit in a frenzy. Because she's desperate, just like me. She's hungry for an orgasm.

I hiss out a breath. I bet waves of pleasure are rolling down her body as her hair grows damp, as her skin heats up, as she rubs that magical device over her aching clit.

The things I could do to help her . . .

Jerking harder, panting faster, I imagine walking into the bathroom right now, stripping off my clothes, and getting under the water. Taking that finger toy and working it on her. Letting her body melt against mine as I get her off, as she begs me to give it to her.

"Chase, it feels so good."

"Chase, I'm dying for you."

"I'm begging you to make me come."

My dick is iron now, and my breath tumbles out in harsh pants as I jack harder and cycle through all the ways I'd make her soar. I'd take over for that vibrator and stroke her sweet clit while I fucked her with my fingers. She'd shatter in my arms.

Tension winds up in my legs, and my quads tighten as I imagine getting her off again, this time with my mouth, feeling her go wild under my tongue. And then I'd push her hands to the tile, slide into that hot, sweet pussy, and play with her magnificent tits as I fucked her until she came again.

Like I'm about to. Holy fuck. I'm about to come so fucking hard because I want that. I want to be the one who turns her inside out with pleasure. I want to be the man she wants fiercely. I'm dying to be the one she gets off to.

A sharp, powerful climax thunders down my spine, lighting me up as I come hard in my hand.

I breathe like a man sprinting, as if I've ridden my bike harder than I ever have. When I open my eyes, I thank the Lord that Josie's paper dedication extends from toilet paper all the way to tissues, because there's a box of Kleenex next to me. I grab some and clean up, then head to the kitchen to wash my hands and readjust my dick.

When the shower turns off, the images haven't stopped. All I can see is her naked, wet, and hungry for me. And I can't stop fucking her in my mind. I can't take my hands off her.

Five minutes later she emerges, her wet hair in a twisty bun. She wears light blue pajama bottoms and a pink tank top. She claps her hands together. "Those seven-layer bars should be ready to eat now," she says, all sweet and innocent.

Soon, we sit down with our glasses of milk and her treats, like a good boy and girl.

As I watch her nibble on a chocolate-chip-covered corner of a bar, I wonder if she was thinking about two unknown guys in the shower.

Or if she's like me, and got off to her roommate.

Chapter Sixteen
From the pages of Josie's Recipe Book

Josie's Magic Amnesiac Seven-Layer Bars

Ingredients

½ cup unsalted butter, melted

1 ½ cups graham cracker crumbs

1 cup finely chopped pecans (can substitute walnuts)

1 cup semisweet chocolate chips

½ cup butterscotch chips

1 cup sweetened flaked coconut

1 (14-ounce) can sweetened condensed milk

When you really need to take your mind off someone, I highly recommend seven-layer bars. The taste is so intoxicatingly delicious that it is quite possibly the closest substitute for . . . Well, look—let's just say these bars are some kind of sublimation.

Directions

1. Preheat oven to 350 degrees. In small bowl, combine graham cracker crumbs and butter; mix well. Press crumb mixture firmly on bottom of baking pan.

Pressing firmly makes me focus all my energy on cooking. Not on how much I'm looking forward to Chase coming home. Not on how much I'm enjoying living with him. Not on how much I liked rubbing his shoulders the other week. Gah. I messed up the recipe. Be right back.

2. Layer in remaining ingredients; press firmly with fork. Pour sweetened condensed milk evenly over crumb mixture.

Baking is therapy. It soothes me. The times when dating in New York City has been weird and frustrating and disappointing, at least there's something I can do well. I can mix and create, and turn ingredients into something tasty. Something that makes people happy. Honestly, I suppose that's all I really want in life. To make someone happy. Even better if that someone makes me feel that way, too.

3. Bake twenty-five minutes or until lightly browned. Cool. Cut into bars.

Serve to your roommate with a straight face as if you didn't just imagine him grabbing you, touching you, sliding into you, and pounding you hard under the hot stream of water in your shower. No, I swear I didn't fantasize about every naked inch of him, and he's not the reason I had to bite my lip to keep from screaming out his name.

4. Have a second helping.

Well, I did say the bars were sublimation.

CHAPTER SEVENTEEN

The red line flattens. Anguish floods my bones. Sorrow drowns my blood.

The patient is gone.

We lost him, a thirty-four-year-old man named Blake Treehorn.

All the medicine, all the paddles, all the speeding ambulances, all the nurses and doctors here at Mercy, and we couldn't save his life.

I exhale heavily. One of the nurses makes the sign of the cross. Another runs her hand gently along the patient's arm. I look at my watch and confirm the time of death.

"One thirty-five p.m.," I say, and the nurse records the information in his chart. I scrub a hand over my jaw as a profound sense of both sadness and failure digs deep into my flesh. I'll be signing his death certificate shortly.

David, another ER doc who worked to save him too, claps me on the back. "We did our best," he mumbles.

"Yeah."

That's the thing. We did. The paramedics barreled in fifteen minutes ago with a man who worked at an office building ten blocks away. During a routine Wednesday afternoon meeting, Blake clutched his chest and complained of pain. He collapsed seconds later, and his coworkers called 911. He'd been fading when he arrived, and we'd fought like hell to save the guy. Thirty minutes later, he's dead in his early thirties on a hospital bed in an emergency room in the middle of Manhattan.

"Life is short, man," David says, his tone heavy.

"It sure is," I say with a sigh.

I've lost patients before. Every doctor has. Last year in Africa, we said good-bye to more people than I wanted to count. It's part of the job. I get that, and I can live with it. It's what I signed up for.

But I'm only human, and I'm not as steel as I pretend to be. This one hits me hard. Blake was young and healthy. I heard one of his coworkers say he'd gone running with him the other morning.

There's no time to sit with these churning emotions, though. When the charge nurse informs me there are multiple gunshot wounds coming in, I have to pretend I'm Teflon.

That's how the rest of the afternoon unfurls. Like a parade of pain and heartache. No sex wounds, no amusing tales, no naughty moments that make for funny stories with friends. It's all too fucking real. One of the gunshot victims dies from blood loss. A patient who seemed to be improving after coming in yesterday with a stroke passes on.

By the time my shift finally ends, I sink down on the bench in the locker room, so ready to be done with the Grim Reaper today. But I just sit. I can't move yet. A leaden weight has settled deep in my gut. I drop my forehead to my hand

and let the gloom spread through me. Sometimes I am good at separating work from my emotions. But sometimes work is emotional. As much as I pride myself on the ability to wear blinders, the fact is my business is one of life and death.

And death sucks.

The door creaks open and David trudges in. "Want to get a beer?"

I raise my face. "Pretty sure you meant whiskey."

A small smile cracks on his tired face. "Make it a double."

"You're on."

And that's how I find myself at Speakeasy in Midtown at five p.m. We trade war stories and talk sports, and it eases some of the day from my shoulders.

When we finish, David tips his chin and pushes his glasses up higher on the bridge of his nose. "And on that note, I should head home to the woman."

I clasp his hand in a good-bye shake, and when I leave, that last word resonates with me. There's one woman I want to see.

Josie closes late on Wednesdays so I catch the subway and exit at Seventy-Second. When I walk along the block where she works, the early evening crowds thickening around me, I swear I can feel the clouds lift and my heart start to lighten just from knowing I'll see her. Josie is my sunshine in this rain-soaked day.

As the smooth, intelligent voice of the audiobook narrator in my ears delves into the physics of perpetual motion, I pass a flower shop, spotting a bouquet of daisies. For the briefest of seconds, an idea takes hold. But I smash it, scoffing at myself. I'm only going to say hi to her. Bringing her flowers would be something one of her cheeseball dates would do. I'm not dating her. I don't have to worry if she'll be in my life tomorrow, or the next day, or the next year. She *is* in my life because she's my friend, and that's why I'm the one who gets to see her, who gets to stop by her work, who gets to hang out with her. The rest of the assholes aren't good enough to even get past a first date.

But she does like flowers.

I stop, turn around, and buy the daisies from her friend Lily's shop. I haven't met Lily before, but the brunette who helps me is sweet and outgoing, so I assume she must be Josie's friend. And I hope she sorts out the situation with her dickhead boyfriend, because whoever he is, he needs to treat her better.

"The flowers are beautiful. Have a great evening," I say, since the least I can do is be a considerate customer.

"You, too," she says with a friendly wave.

I leave the store.

As I near Josie's bakery, a whole squadron of nerves launches in my chest. My heart speeds up. This doesn't just feel like nerves from the day. This feels like something else entirely. Something I haven't felt in a long time. Something that's good, but terribly dangerous at the same damn time.

Gripping the bouquet tighter, I push open the yellow door to the Sunshine Bakery. Josie works alone, bending to take a huge slice of chocolate cake from the glass counter. She stands, sets it in a white bakery box, and hands it to the customer, a thin redhead wearing jeans and heels. The customer rubs her hands together. "I can't wait. This is my favorite cake in all of New York City."

Josie tilts her head and flashes the woman a wide, genuine smile. "I'm so happy to hear that. You deserve a slice today," she says, then tells her the amount.

Josie's hair is swept back in a pink-checked bandana, her bangs showing. Her T-shirt is orange, with the cheery sun logo of her store. Bangles slip and slide on her wrist. When the customer leaves, Josie's eyes find mine, and they light up.

"Hey you!" she calls out and slinks around the counter to give me a hug. We don't usually hug when we see each other, but maybe her arms are around me because I don't stop by her work that often. Or maybe she senses that I need it.

"Hey," I say, then I steal a quick inhale. Today she is cake. She is frosting. She is sugar and everything good in the world, and all those strange sensations descend on me once more as my heart beats weirdly faster.

When we separate, she arches an eyebrow. "What brings you to these environs, stranger? I'm about to close up."

I clear my throat and thrust the flowers at her.

Her smile grows even bigger. She dips her nose to the petals and inhales. "I love them. My favorite."

"I know."

"I'm going to take them home. To make our place cheery," she says as she heads to the door, locks it, and flips the sign to say "Closed."

When she turns around to meet my gaze, I sink down at one of the tables and drag a hand through my hair.

"Uh-oh," she says, joining me and setting down the bouquet. "Bad day at work?"

I nod.

She brings her chair even closer. "I'm guessing that means a real bad day, not a bad day like someone-at-the-hospital-ate-your-tuna-fish-sandwich-in-the-break-room-fridge bad day?"

"I hate tuna fish sandwiches."

She laughs. "Me, too." She takes a beat. "Tell me what happened."

So I do.

And when I'm done, I feel a hell of a lot better, and lighter, and happier than I did after having drinks with David. No disrespect to the dude. He's a cool cat.

But he's not Josie, and she's quickly become the person I want to talk to.

Scratch that. She's been that person for a long time.

Especially since she's a great listener, and she has access to much better medicine than I do some days. The strawberry shortcake cupcake I eat as we walk home can cure almost any sadness.

* * *

Later, I lie awake in bed.

Darkness has fallen over our home. Moonlight cuts through the blinds, casting stripes of light over the navy bedspread. Outside, a horn bleats and a garbage truck slogs along the avenue, lifting and dumping, lifting and dumping.

I flip to my side, the sheets slipping to my waist.

The green lights on the clock flash 11:55 at me.

But I can't fall asleep easily like I usually do. I can't blame the events at Mercy. I've had to let them go. Tomorrow is another day, and I need to be sharp for whatever comes my way. I'm not a superstitious man, but bad news comes in waves, so I need to be girded for a possible roulette wheel of destruction tomorrow.

So it's not the patients—may Blake, and the gunshot guy, too, rest in peace—that I'm thinking of anymore.

It's the woman on the other side of this wall. What's keeping me up is the part of me that insisted on seeing her at the end of the day. The part that demanded I go to Sunshine Bakery, that I buy her flowers, that I tell her what happened.

I squeeze my eyes closed, imagining a patient is presenting with the same symptoms I have. What would I conclude?

I list them in my head—heart beating faster unexpectedly, nerves appearing incon-fucking-veniently, desire to see the woman after a shitty day.

When I get to the last one, I stop. On *desire*. Because there's the embodiment of it in my doorway.

In shadows, she stands. She raises her hand and waves. "Hey," she says softly.

"Hey."

"You awake?"

"No. I'm sound asleep."

She laughs and leans her shoulder against the doorframe. She's in her usual asleep attire. Boy shorts, like the kind you'd find in a Victoria's Secret catalogue. Material as thin as a spider web, and just as wispy. She pairs them with a loose pink scoop-neck shirt. No bra.

I'm so fucking screwed.

I prop my head in my hand. "I thought you were the queen sleeper. What's the story there? Insomnia visiting you?"

She quirks her lips. Holds out her hands. "Lot on my mind."

I push up higher. "Yeah?"

She fidgets with the hem of her shirt. "I keep thinking about your day." Then she rolls her eyes. "You know me. Everything is all mushed together."

"Like cake batter, huh?"

She nods. "I'm all blended," she says, then mimes mixing up some goodies.

"Do you want to . . . talk?"

"I don't want to keep you up."

"I'm already up."

Her eyes drift to my bed. My breath escapes my body. Shit. Fuck. Hell. Heaven. There's no excuse for what I'm about to do. But I do it anyway.

I pat my bed.

A small lift of her lips is her answer.

Then a step forward. Her bare feet pad across my floor. Every moment is a chance to turn back. But every moment she comes closer.

And closer.

And now she lowers herself to my bed. She's barely wearing anything. I'm only in briefs. She lies on top of the sheets. I'm under them. But she's inches away.

Technically, I can play my mind games with myself. I can rationalize this choice in a simple, logical way. We're still dressed. A sheet separates us. She lies on her back. I'm propped on my side.

But the moonlight, and the hour, and this aching in my chest won't let me lie to myself anymore.

I'm buzzed.

I'm totally fucking tipsy on the possibility. We've hugged, we've touched, we've been like two middle-schoolers tapping shoulders and tickling waists.

Tonight, we're adults in bed.

"I was thinking about your patient tonight." Her tone is introspective. "You said Blake was thirty-four. And the heart attack was out of the blue. I'm only twenty-eight."

"You're not going to have a heart attack, Josie."

"Right. I know. I mean, I think I won't. I don't eat too many treats," she says with a twinkle in her eyes. Her hand drifts to her belly, and she pats it. "I mean, maybe a few more than I should."

"Stop it. You're beautiful," I say before I can think better of it.

She arches a brow. "Really?"

"Yes."

"I could lose five pounds. Maybe ten."

I roll my eyes. "If you lost five pounds, you wouldn't be you. You're a baker. No one wants a skinny baker. And trust me, wherever these five or ten pounds are that you want to lose, I don't want to see them gone."

She smiles. "Thank you. The funny thing is, I think I'd regret not tasting and sampling the things I make more than I'd enjoy being five pounds lighter. So, honestly, I'm happy with my five or ten extra, I suppose. I feel like at the end of my life, whether it's at age thirty-four or ninety or twenty-nine, I won't be saying, 'I wish I ate less cake.' Or 'I wish I had fewer seven-layer bars.' And I don't think I'll be saying, 'I should have spent more time on Facebook or Twitter or Snapchat,' either."

I laugh. Josie's hardly online. She's social, but she's social in real life. "What would you regret?"

She shifts closer and props her head in her hand, mirroring me. The space between us is endless, and at the same time, it barely exists. Maybe six or seven inches separate us. Few enough for me to loop my fingers in her hair, tug her close, and kiss the hell out of her. But more than enough for me to *not* cross that line, too.

Lines. Friendship. Having her in my life. Living with her. Those reasons ought to be enough to stay on this side of the kiss/don't kiss divide.

"I'm not sure I'd regret anything," she says. "I'm trying to live a life without regrets. I'm glad I took over the bakery. I'm glad I took out the loan. I'm glad I pursued my dreams. I'm even glad I'm doing the whole online-dating thing," she says, and my heart sinks like a stone.

"Yeah?"

"I'd like to find the one. I'd like to fall in love. I'd like to have a family and all that jazz."

"You would?"

She nods. "I would. I try to do the things that matter to me so I won't have regrets. Do you have any regrets?"

I flop to my back, reflecting on her question. "I've done the things I want to do so far. The things that are important to me. So, honestly, aside from you using my hand as Lyle Lyle, I can't really think of a thing I regret not doing," I say, deadpan all the way.

She's silent, and I look over at her.

A smile spreads slowly across her pretty face. Her green eyes twinkle with mischief, and her soft, sweet lips lift into a sexy grin.

Then she flips to her side, her back to me, and slides under the sheets. She scoots closer. I take that as my cue to spoon her.

I've drunk too much champagne. I've eaten too much dessert. I'm in bed with Josie Hammer, her sweet, sexy body pressed to mine, and she reaches for my hand.

I slide it over her shirt and between her breasts, and I groan.

I've finally become a stuffed crocodile, and it's better than all my fantasies.

She sighs, the kind of sleepy nighttime sigh of contentment that comes from a woman who's living a life without regret. I'd like to think I am, too. But when she falls asleep a minute later in my arms, I do regret something.

I regret that I'm completely and utterly unable to resist my best friend.

I press a soft kiss to the back of her neck, and I'm certain I can't stay on this side of the divide anymore.

Chapter Eighteen

I must have fallen asleep, too.

But when I wake up, it feels as if I'm still dreaming. My arms are wrapped around her, and my hand is wedged between the two most beautiful breasts I've ever felt.

But it's not my hand that is doing the most interesting thing.

Not at all.

Her hand is on my hip.

She's stroking me. She's touching me. She's running her fingers from my hip, down the outside of my leg.

This is the best dream I've ever had.

Her breath catches, and then the dream ratchets up. It goes to dream level twenty or fifty or ten million when she presses her ass against my dick. She pushes back lightly, and then a soft moan falls from her lips.

Ohhhh.

It's the sexiest sound I've ever heard.

And I surrender to it.

"Josie," I whisper, my voice raspy.

"Mmm," she murmurs.

"Turn around, baby."

The sheets rustle, and then we're face-to-face. I lift my hand, cup her cheek, and brush my thumb along her jaw. Then I kiss her, and holy fucking hell. I'm on fire in seconds. I'm lit up everywhere. Sparks, and desire, and lust—they all just fucking combust the second our lips touch.

My fingers slide into her hair, and her hand slinks up my bare chest, and I kiss her without holding back. No reservations. No regrets.

My tongue sweeps across hers, and she deepens the kiss, seeking more. She kisses me back with a raw hunger. Her lips are eager, and she explores mine just like I do to hers. It's a hand-off, a back and forth. I lead, then she leads, then we both kiss greedily, and we can't seem to get enough. I don't want to stop because she tastes so fucking good, and she turns me on so fucking much, and I want her more than I've ever wanted anyone.

And in mere seconds of kissing her, I can already tell how she'll be in bed—how she's give-and-take. Her hands travel up and down my chest, her nails scratch at my pecs, and her fingertips outline my abs. My hand curls around the back of her skull, holding her tight as I kiss her hard, sucking on her bottom lip, then the top, then just devouring her mouth.

I push her shoulders down to the bed, and we're no longer side to side. She's on her back, and I know where she wants me. I know where I want to be.

Her hand tugs at my hip and I move on top of her, and then I'm so far fucking gone. Because she spreads her legs. I grab her thigh, hook it around my hip, and then grind against her.

Yeah, I'm dry humping her. And it's fucking astonishing. I kiss and thrust, and she moans and arches. She kisses me with her whole body, and it makes my head swim with lust. I'm dying, fucking dying to be inside her.

I'm so goddamn hard, and she's already ridiculously wet. I can feel her damp panties through these flimsy shorts that I want to tear off her. But I don't want to break contact—I just want to fuck Josie like this.

When she matches a rough thrust of mine, a white-hot charge of pleasure surges down my spine, and I stop the kiss. I'm not in danger of firing early, but I can't hold back what's on my mind.

She stares up at me with dazed eyes. I grab her chin, hold her face firmly. "You okay with all this?" I ask, my voice tight. I have to know. I need to make sure she's good with what's happening.

"Completely," she says, her voice as certain as my desire.

I sigh, and it's full of fucking gratitude that she's on the same page. I stare into her eyes and say what I've longed to tell her. "I want you so much."

It's not poetry. It's not even the kind of filthy smut that probably wins awards wherever awards are handed out for that. But I don't care. It's the truth, plain and simple.

"I want you, too, Chase," she says.

Her answer is my greatest wish.

Letting go of her chin, I drop my face to her neck, sucking on her flesh. The scent of her cherry lotion floods my nostrils, and I'm getting high. She's fucking cocaine to me, and God, I want more. It's euphoric, it's electric, the rush I get from smelling her, from moving against her, from kissing her.

"God, you smell so good," I growl. "Do you have any idea what it's like having you as a roommate when you go around smelling like that?"

She laughs lightly, and at the same time she tightens her legs around my ass. "How do I smell?"

"Like cherries, and sex, and cake, and all I have to do is take one whiff of you and I'm rock-hard," I say, thrusting against her to prove my point.

She moans, stretching her neck. "You are rock-hard, and I love it. And I love that you're turned on, because it's the same for me with you." She grabs my face, holding me as she grinds up into my dick. "I sniffed your shaving cream the other day."

My eyes widen. "You did?"

"You weren't home. I opened the medicine cabinet. I smelled it and I shivered." Then she lowers her voice even more. "And it made me wet just thinking of you."

Lust rattles through my bones. I swivel my hips and grind against her through all these stupid clothes. "You were that aroused?"

"God, yes," she moans as she lets go of my face, her hands darting around to grab my ass.

"When you tugged at that towel, I fucking went crazy," I say, and the admissions are rolling out, rattling free, spilling everywhere.

"The other morning?"

I nod as I push against her.

She gasps. "Oh God, please. I think I'm going to come like this," she says, and that's a battle cry if I ever heard one. I heed it. I fuck her with clothes on. She moans, and groans, and cries out. Somehow she spreads her legs wider, and then she just rocks up into me, finding a perfect rhythm against the outline of my cock.

As I thrust, I kiss her neck, travel to her ear, and nip on her earlobe. I want to hear every moan she makes up close. I want her noises in stereo. I want to drown in the sounds of her coming, in her *yes*, and *oh God*, and *so close*.

She digs her nails into my ass and rocks up into me. I love that she's found what she needs. That my dick, even through clothes, is enough friction to get her off.

And when she goes, it's like an explosion. She cries out. She moans. She writhes. And she warns me. Like I need it.

"I'm coming, oh God, I'm coming, oh my fucking God, I'm fucking coming."

What a smoking, filthy, wonderfully dirty mouth she has. Her lips fall into an *O* and her eyes squeeze shut. Pleasure and torment mix exquisitely on her beautiful face. I don't even try to separate anything anymore. I'm so fucking lost in her. I don't pretend. I don't want to. I can't do anything but stare in awe at the glory of Josie coming beneath me in my bed.

"Oh God, oh God, oh God," she says, panting and moaning as she starts to come down. She breathes out hard and each exhalation sounds like pure satisfaction.

Then she laughs. A giggle at first. As it turns into a chuckle, I arch a brow. "Something funny?"

She shakes her head and opens her eyes. They're glossy with lust and brimming with satisfaction. "No, I'm laughing because it was so good."

I flash her a lopsided grin as pride surges through me. "Yeah?"

She loops her arms around my neck and tugs me down, bringing my mouth to hers and kissing me. When she breaks the kiss, she says, "Yeah, Chase. It was the definition of mind-blowing."

I wiggle an eyebrow.

And then her busy little hand darts between us, shooting down to my briefs. She cups my dick, and I'm not even sure I can ever speak again. Words fail me. There is nothing as good as Josie touching me when I'm on the edge already.

She whistles, a low appreciative sound. "Nice package, Summers."

What can I say? I wasn't shortchanged when dicks were handed out.

Then she lets go, pushes on my chest, and knocks me to my back. In a second, I'm pinned. She straddles me, dropping down on my cock, rubbing against me. Her little shorts are damp, soaked all the way through. Grabbing my wrists, she pins them over my head—such a fierce little thing. Straddling me, she rocks back and forth, and holy shit, my roommate is a wild lover. She's daring and unafraid, and she wants me. It floors me, the look in her eyes—all heat and fire, her green irises like blazing emeralds.

She lowers her face near mine, her hair falling like a curtain, framing me in more of her wondrous scent. God, when did I become so addicted to the way someone smelled? I don't have a clue, but it's happened with her.

"Chase," she whispers, and for a second I tense, thinking she's going to want to talk about what we're doing. I don't want to discuss or dissect it. But we're on the same wavelength because she says, "Want to know what else gets me off?"

My throat goes dry. "Yes. I do."

A little thrust of her hips. "Want to know what did it for me in the shower the other night?"

I strain against her wrists. I want to touch her so badly, but I can tell she wants to steer this ship. "I'm dying to know," I rasp out, my voice like a dry husk on a hot summer day.

Then the vixen runs her tongue over her teeth, brings her mouth to my earlobe, and whispers, "The thought of sucking your cock."

I'm roasted. I'm fried. I'm well past broiled. I push against her hands, sit up, cup her cheeks, and stare into her eyes.

"Do it," I tell her.

She nibbles on the corner of her lip and shoots me a wicked grin. She's like a quick fox, darting down, her hands tugging at the waistband of my boxers. She yanks them off, my dick springing free.

She kneels between my legs and takes my cock in her hand. She's silent for a moment. When she speaks, her words are the best dirty poetry. "You're fucking beautiful," she says, staring at me as if she's mesmerized. And she's not looking at my face. She's gazing at my dick, and I couldn't be happier that she's bestowing compliments on that part of my anatomy.

She wraps her hand tighter and strokes up once, and it feels out-of-this-world good. I shudder. She bends lower and licks.

"Holy fuck," I mutter, my head falling back onto the pillow. It's so ridiculously good.

She swirls her tongue over the head, licking me as if I'm a piece of candy and making the sexiest murmurs.

"Fuck, that's good, baby."

She wraps her lips nice and tight and inches lower, taking more. The pleasure in me shoots into the atmosphere, sails above the stratosphere.

I don't want to go crazy and fuck her mouth hard, but God, I want to go crazy and fuck her mouth hard. I lace my hands in her hair and thrust up into her heavenly mouth, letting her lead, letting her take what she can.

She takes it all, sucks me to the base, and then licks her way back up. She drives me insane.

"Jesus fucking Christ," I say, and when I stare down, she's smiling, she's fucking grinning, and her eyes meet mine. They're full of both mischief and utter, sensual delight.

My God. *This woman.* This amazing woman.

She picks up the pace, and her mouth is a blur. My vision is, too, and my whole body sizzles. It crackles. It pops. It's ready to snap. I'm losing control, and an orgasm gathers force in my body as her mouth races over my dick. When she wraps her hand around my shaft, squeezing the base, I fire.

Unspeakable pleasure barrels through me from a climax so powerful it rocks me to my bones.

I grunt and grip her head, my hands curling tighter as I come in her mouth, and my whole world turns electric with ecstasy.

At some point the orgasm recedes, but I'm still floating because that was the kind of orgasm you could measure on the Richter scale. It's the kind that makes the news. That causes epic aftershocks. I tremble as another wave ripples through me.

With a loud, wet pop, she lets go of my dick, wipes her hand over her mouth, and crawls up my body. "You tasted better than you did in the shower."

I kiss her, and she seems surprised at first, like who would kiss a girl who just went down on him? *This guy.* She kisses me back harder, and when we separate, I say, "I want to do that to you."

"I want that, too."

I cup her cheek. "I want to sleep with you, Josie. I want to be inside you. God, I want you so much there aren't enough Swedish Fish to explain it."

"I want you, too," she says, then dusts a light kiss on my lips. "But I'm not ready tonight."

And I don't know what that means, except the obvious—this isn't a one-time thing.

CHAPTER NINETEEN

She's up and gone before I even wake up.

It's probably for the best.

Not that I don't want to see her.

More like all I want is to see her, but I don't know what we're supposed to say or do, or how we're supposed to act after last night.

Do I just bump into her on the way into the bathroom to brush my teeth and say "hey," all nonchalant? Or do we wake up and pepper each other's cheeks with morning smooches?

I drag my ass out of bed, grateful I don't have to make those decisions this morning. After I shower, dress, and grab my phone, I head for the door.

I stop.

And stare.

And grin.

On the doorknob hangs a black lace thong, like she promised she'd leave if she expected to be getting it on. But that was when we'd first laid out our roommate rules. When we didn't expect to be getting it on with each other. Truth be told, though, I can recall a dose of jealousy coursing through me during that conversation at the mere prospect of her with someone else.

Hell, maybe this thing between us started before I was even aware of it.

I grab the scrap of lacy fabric, twirl it on my finger, and then bring it to my nose. It smells fresh and clean, like her laundry detergent. I toy with the idea of stuffing it into my pocket, but I'm not a panty-stuffer—or even a habitual panty-sniffer, for that matter.

Instead, I leave it on the coffee table, and I look for a sheet of paper to write her a note when I spot something else from her.

A small, see-through plastic bag from her bakery with a sunshine yellow ribbon wrapped around it. Inside are red candies. A little bakery card dangles from the ribbon. I flick it open and read.

Are things supposed to be awkward now between us? Or weird? Or tense? I hope not. But just in case . . . here's some Swedish Fish, and the hope for more.

My heart thumps harder than it should from a gift of candy. But it's not just candy. It's the perfect morning-after acknowledgement. It's everything I wanted to say last night, but couldn't. It's her knowing how to fucking handle this.

And it's one more thing that makes me want her in every way.

I ride my bike to the hospital, whipping through the early-morning traffic like nothing can get me down. And nothing can. Because something is happening. Something wild, and crazy, and undoubtedly incredibly foolish.

138 · LAUREN BLAKELY

But right now, it feels so fucking good, like sailing, like flying, like soaring.

* * *

Chase: Can't. Stop. Thinking. About. You.

Josie: Ditto. Ditto. Ditto.

Chase: Love the panties.

Josie: Thought you might.

Chase: Love the fish. I ate them all when I walked into work. Totally got jacked up on a sugar high before I had to put stitches in a chin. Some dude fell off his skateboard.

Josie: Ouch. But maybe you've uncovered some new natural high for a physician!

Chase: Ha, maybe I have. Also, most of all, love the note. A lot. I'm curious, though. Did you just happen to have candy on hand?

Josie: Perhaps I did. Perhaps I had them on hand just for this occasion.

Chase: More later. Forceps calling my name. But that is awesome.

Josie: Good luck, Doctor McHottie. When you're done with whatever emergency has your name on it, here's this treat for you.

A picture fills my screen, and I stop in the hospital corridor, grab the wall, and try to snap my tongue back up from the floor. Because I am panting *that* hard as I gawk at the image of the tops of her breasts. She took a goddamn fucking selfie of her tits, and I'm royally turned on.

But here at work, I have to keep the drawers neat, so I turn off my phone. I'm all business for the two hours until break time.

* * *

Chase: Had to remove a marble from a nose, and it took all my brainpower not to think of the sad fact that I didn't get to see your breasts in the flesh last night. Your picture didn't help. Wait. Scratch that. Send more. SHOW THEM ALL TO ME.

Chase: I should let you know I'm a dirty bastard, and you have the world's most glorious breasts I've ever seen, only I haven't seen them yet. Therefore, I'm sad.

Josie: Don't be sad. I have a solution to make you happy.

Chase: More pictures???

Josie: Better. I'll flash you when you get home.

Chase: Did you just hear the groan of excitement I made all the way from Mercy?

Josie: It's still reverberating here in the Upper West Side.

Chase: Also, please do more than flash me.

Chase: Gotta go. Break's over. See ya.

Josie: Good luck. Let me know if you want me to bring you home anything.

Chase: You.

CHAPTER TWENTY

Max lowers the hood on an electric-blue beauty, gently closing it. His eyes are focused on the metal meeting metal the entire time, until it's whisper-quiet on the lot. Then he turns, wipes his hands on a red-checked rag, and nods hello.

"What will that sapphire baby set me back?" I tip my chin toward the sleek vehicle that shines so bright it's reflecting the skyscrapers nearby where Max's custom car shop is located in Midtown West.

He laughs at me and shakes his head. "More than you ever can afford," he says, then tucks the rag into the back pocket of his jeans, streaked with grease.

He's shirtless, the fucking show-off. "Dude, put a shirt on."

"You can't handle this much manliness, can you?"

He puffs out his chest, the intricate Celtic tats on his pec and the tribal bands on his arms on full display.

I roll my eyes. "Let's just say I see more bodies naked in a day than you can even imagine, and though most aren't vying for Centerfold of the Month, yours still ranks as the one I least want to see bare."

In a flurry, Max wraps an arm around me and puts me in a headlock.

Fuck, I forgot how strong he is. His muscle-bound bicep ropes tighter around me, and he digs his knuckles into my head, reminding me how he's the master at noogies.

"Say you love me best," Max commands, his voice deep. "My bare chest especially."

I wince as his grip tightens. I refuse to give in. "Never," I grunt.

"You sure?" His knuckles might, just might, be penetrating my skull now. He's sweaty, too. Crap. I have to give in.

Nope. I can't give in.

"I love you but not your chest," I say between stilted breaths.

The punishment deepens. He squeezes harder. Airflow becomes a debatable item in my life. I have no choice. "And your stupid chest," I mutter.

"My chest isn't stupid."

His hold on me turns pincer-grip style, but his skin is sweaty from work, and with one quick twist I break free, then dart out from his grip. Thrusting both hands in the air, I strut across the asphalt. "And speed beats brawn," I tease.

Max just shakes his head at me as he strides inside the garage and grabs a black T-shirt from his messy desk, strewn with papers and tools.

He tugs the shirt on and wipes his brow. He returns to the small lot. "And the answer is—this baby is a cool five hundred K," he says, running his hand lovingly along the exterior of the car.

I whistle. "Damn. What have you Frankensteined together here?"

"It's a souped-up Lambo, and get this—" His dark brown eyes gleam with excitement. "Got a call earlier today about custom outfitting a car for RBC network for a new show where the hero is like a modern-day Magnum, P.I."

"Fuck yeah," I say, clasping his hand in a congratulatory shake. "That's awesome."

"It'll be a blast and it should do wonders for business," he says and mimes an explosion with his hands. Max's business is already killing it, and he's got several celebrity clients as well as plenty of under-the-radar high-rollers. "But this kind of deal could be huge for publicity."

"You are a rock star," I say, no joking, no teasing this time. "You ready to ride?"

"Always," he says, since we're scheduled for a training ride before I head home. Josie has her soccer league tonight, so I'm not sure when I'll see her.

He heads inside to grab his road bike, and while he's gone my phone beeps.

I grab it from my back pocket.

Josie: Game over. We crushed the competition.

Chase: Because you're fucking fierce on the field.

Josie: That might be true. :) Okay, catching the subway. Heading home. How was your day?

Before I tap out a reply, I answer the question in my head. My day was fucking amazing. My day was fantastic. My day was the best ever. Because of last night.

But more so, because of where I want to be right now. Where she is.

I drop the mic.

That's it.

Everything's clear.

I know. I just fucking know.

She's the one I want to spend the rest of this day with. She's the one I want to talk to about my good days and my bad days. She's more than my roommate. She's more than one of my best friends. She's the one I want every day. I have no clue what happens after tonight, but I need tonight with her to start right the fuck now.

When Max rolls out on his bike, I point my thumb across town. "I gotta bail."

"What?" he asks, like this doesn't compute.

"You were right."

"I always am. But about what this time?"

"Just say I told you so. Just go ahead and say it."

"I told you so?" he tosses out quizzically.

"You did. And I have to go see Josie. Wait. No. Correction. I *want* to go see Josie."

Max snickers and shoots me the biggest I-told-you-so grin in the history of facial expressions.

I shrug. What can you do? Then I go to the only place I want to be.

The diagnosis I was trying to piece together last night? All the symptoms point to one malady.

I've got it bad for this girl. I've got a textbook condition of a classic illness. I'm suffering from a motherfucking case of falling in love.

And I'm not ready to take a pill to cure it.

CHAPTER TWENTY-ONE

It's a scene ripped straight from a fantasy I never knew I had. But it's so incredibly enticing that the vision in front of me has shot straight up the ranks.

We're talking the Pantheon of dirty images, and it's not even filthy.

Yet.

Josie's in the kitchen, wearing an apron and heels. Her hair is twisted in a bun with a chopstick stabbed through it. A home-cooked meal sits cooling on the rack on the stovetop. I've never had naughty housewife fantasies, but I think I might now.

The apartment smells like my favorite food ever, the one I missed most in Africa—pizza pie with cheese and mushrooms.

An '80s tune, "Tempted" by Squeeze, is playing. If I stop to think about it, the lyrics are wildly wrong. It's technically a song about straying. But I'm convinced this song became famous because all you hear in this tune is the longing, the want, the hunger for another person. That's the thing about song lyrics. You take the parts that speak to you.

Temptation talks loud and clear to me.

Temptation shakes her butt to the beat.

Lord help me.

This.

When the door falls shut behind me with a loud snap, Josie startles and swivels around. She brings her hand to her chest. "Oh God, you scared me."

"Sorry," I say, dropping my keys on the table by the door.

She grabs her phone from the counter and lowers the volume. "Hey," she says, setting the cell down as I enter the tiny kitchen. "I made you a—"

I crush her mouth to mine before she can say "pizza." A sexy *ohh* escapes her lips, and then she gives me all I want.

Her.

She loops her hands around my neck, her fingers traveling up to my hair, playing with the ends. Lust charges down my spine. I sweep my lips across hers, our mouths connecting as we find the rhythm that makes this kiss its own kind of sexy song. I can't break it down to the melody or the lyrics, the notes or the chords. All I know is, this kiss has all the makings of a number-one hit. It has that certain something. That indefinable quality that hooks you right in the heart, hits you hard in the chest and sends the heat levels to incendiary.

Backing her up a few inches to the counter, I slam my body against hers. A sharp, sexy gasp falls from her lips as I break the kiss.

"Hey you," I whisper hungrily.

"Nice to see you, too," she says, then pulls me back to her, our lips crashing together once more. My hands dive into her hair, and I rip the chopstick out, letting those soft brown strands spill over my fingers as the wooden stick clatters to the floor.

As I kiss her, my mind goes hazy, and I shove aside all thoughts of anything but lust and want and heat. Clasping her face in my hands, I kiss her even harder, even hungrier, until I can't take just kissing her. I have to have more of her.

All of her.

When I break the kiss, she's panting. Her hair is a wild mess. Her lips are swollen and red, almost bruised. Her green eyes shine with desire. She's never looked hotter than she does right now. My eyes roam down her body. Her apron is light blue, with a cherry pattern on it. She wears a skirt under it, and the dark red material lands right above her knees.

Underneath the apron is some kind of strappy little white tank top. Brushing my hands along her arms, I watch her shiver.

"This apron . . ." I say, fingering the hem.

"Yeah?"

My hands dart up to her chest, then around her neck where it ties. But I don't undo the knot. "There's something I'm curious about."

"What is it?"

As I fiddle playfully with the straps, I meet her eyes. "I can't stop wondering how you'd look in just this apron on top."

Her lips curve up in a naughty grin, and she reaches behind her. The little ping of a clasp coming undone lands on my ears, and I groan. She's freeing her breasts from their confines. My body hums with anticipation. I lick my lips as I watch every move she makes. Now her hands slide up to her shoulders, and she performs something that looks a lot like circus acrobatics to me, but it's one of those things girls can do blindfolded. She tugs one slim bra strap down her right arm and off. The other slides down her left arm. Then she slips her hands under her apron again and tells me to close my eyes. Dutifully, I oblige.

Fifteen seconds later, she says, "Open them."

When I do, the white tank is pooled on the floor, and she holds up a lacy white bra, letting it dangle from her index finger. The apron top still covers her. "Is this what you wanted?"

"That is exactly what I wanted."

I take the bra, toss it into the other room, and grab her hips. I lift her up on the counter and drink in the view.

Skirt, heels, and apron. Her breasts are barely covered, and for a man obsessed with breasts, you'd think I'd be fondling them right now. But I'm also not twelve. I want to savor the view. I want to admire my girl. I want to experience every fucking glorious second of this night, imprint it all on my brain, feed every memory cell I have.

I reach around her neck and tug at the apron tie. Her breath catches, and she trembles. A shudder runs through her body.

It gives me pause. "You okay?" I ask, because I can't not. "Are you cold?"

"No, I'm good. Just very, very good," she says, tipping up her chin. Her eyes meet mine, and in a flash I see so much vulnerability, so much longing in them, it nearly knocks me to my knees. It almost makes me want to spill my whole heart to her, to tell her what I realized at Max's garage. But if there's a recipe for killing a friendship, that's it, right there. When you add love to the mix—when you openly declare it—you might as well say good-bye to the friendship. We can be friends and we can have benefits, but anything more is playing with fire. I know this, and she surely does, too.

Tonight, we're lovers.

That's what I zone in on as I undo the apron tie.

The knot loosens. The straps slide. The fabric ties fall down her chest.

Dear God, she's gorgeous. Her breasts are as magnificent as I imagined. Soft, creamy, gorgeous globes with rosy nipples, tipped up. I bend to her chest, draw one delicious peak into my mouth, and suck.

"Oh God," she moans, and her hands grab the back of my head, clutching me tight.

Just when I think a moment can't be more perfect, it proves me wrong.

This is beyond compare.

I cup the other breast in my left hand, squeezing, then pinching her nipple as I suck. A throaty groan meets my ears, then an anguished "please," chased by a breathy "God, that's so good."

Yes, it's so good. It's so fucking good. It's absolutely fucking amazingly exquisite to have my face buried between Josie's tits. I could spend the next day, or week, or month here. In fact, when Mercy comes looking for me because I missed my next several shifts, they'll find me squirreled away in the land of absolute bliss.

Here.

I make no apologies for my obsession. I don't consider this a guilty pleasure, either, because I don't feel a shred of guilt about something that drives both of us crazy. Judging from the way her fingers are locked around my skull, Josie loves the attention I'm lavishing on her chest as much as I love giving it. Her breath comes fast, and her hips wriggle on the counter as I lick and suck and kiss her breasts. She moans and sighs and murmurs.

At some point, maybe in the next century, I wrestle myself away and meet her gaze. I don't let go of these beauties, though. I fondle them as I look at her, all flushed and sexy.

"Jesus Christ, Josie," I say, just in awe of *her*. Everything. How she looks at me. How her lips fall open. How her eyes are guileless. The way she inches closer to me.

"I'm in love with—" I catch myself before I screw things up with her. "Your tits. They're fucking perfect. I hope you don't mind my adoration of them." I flash her a lopsided grin.

She laughs. "I don't mind it at all, and I'll give you free rein with them if you do something for me."

"Name it."

She brings her hand to my chin, pulls me close, and then dusts kisses along my jawline that drive me insane. My dick is knocking on the door of my jeans, begging to be free.

She finds my ear and whispers, "I'm dying for you to go down on me, but I want you to fuck me more."

I groan. "That's so fucking sexy what you just said."

"Is that a yes?"

I adopt a frown. "Why can't I have both?"

She runs her finger over my bottom lip. "You can. But right now," she says, wriggling closer, "I need you inside me."

And that's it.

Done.

Ready.

The woman has asked, and the woman shall receive. I push up her skirt to her waist, shaking my head. "I should be devouring your pussy right now. You distracted me with your perfect tits, so I had no time to go down on you. And then, what do you do to me? You ask me to fuck you. Which is basically the hottest thing in the entire universe."

She laughs. "I like asking for what I want. It turns me on."

I slide my hands under her skirt. "I like it, too, knowing what you want. And I love when you ask. Though, I can also tell . . ."

My eyes roam to her legs, to that decadent land at the apex of her thighs. She's soaked. Her panties are so wet, it's nearly criminal. And I'm a cocky bastard because pride surges in me. I did this—I got her *this* turned on. I love that she's so aroused from the way we kiss and touch and grope that she's soaked through. I drag a finger across the wet panel, and she shudders against me.

As I slide off her panties, she grabs the hem of my T-shirt and yanks it over my head. Then her hands are on my jeans, tugging at the button.

"Damn, woman."

"I want you," she says, firmly. "I want you now."

"Trust me, baby. You're going to have me. And I'm going to make it so fucking good for you. But first we need this." I dip my hand to my back pocket, grab my wallet, and take out a condom. "Hope you don't think I'm a cheapskate, but I got it at work."

She laughs. "One of the perks of working at a hospital." She wraps her arms around my neck and tugs me close. Her eyes are intense. "Say you got it today."

"I absolutely fucking did," I whisper. "Because all day long I've been thinking about how much I want to fuck you."

"Me, too. So much." Her hands go lower and she pushes my jeans over my ass, freeing my dick.

"Put it on me, baby. I know you want to."

"Oh God, I do," she says, panting hard. "I want to touch you so badly."

I'm not sure how I knew she'd be game to wrap me up, but I just did. I'm learning her quickly. Figuring her out. I open the condom wrapper and hand it to her.

As she takes it out, I grab my cock in my hand and rub.

It's like an injection of lust straight into Josie. "Oh God," she moans, her pitch rising as she stares at me. "Stop. You're making me crazy."

"Then it's working." Because crazy is how I want her. Insane with lust. And I don't stop. I fist my hand around my dick, and stroke down to the head, squeezing. Her breath catches, and she groans. Her mouth falls open.

She watches me with wild abandon. Already, I'm thinking of all the things I want to do with her, all the ways I want to fuck her. All the pleasure I want to give her.

She bites the corner of her lip as she removes the condom, then she wraps a hand around my dick and joins in. That desperation in her eyes is replaced by excitement, by some kind of thrill as she holds my cock and I let go.

"Watch me," she says.

And I do, staring at her pretty hands as she slides the protection over my cock, pinching the tip of the latex, making sure it's perfect. And now I'm the one on fire.

Or maybe we both are.

I grab her hips, pull her to the edge of the counter, and rub the tip against her sweet, slippery pussy.

She moans my name. It sounds like a dirty, filthy word from her lips. She says it like it has five syllables, and she wants to be fucked by every single one.

I push in.

"Holy fuck," I groan, because she feels so good.

"I know," she murmurs, and I fucking love that we're on the same page.

Her wetness welcomes me, and it is paradise inside Josie. She's snug, hot, and wet, and she clenches tightly around me as I fill her. Her hands slide up my chest and she grips my shoulders. I brace one hand on the counter, the other on her hip as I nestle deep inside her.

I thrust and she cries out.

I groan as I move inside her, taking my time at first, then I fuck her on the kitchen counter. Because I can't wait. Sure, I can wait to go down on her. Yes, I can wait to carry her to the bedroom. I can even wait for dinner. But I can't wait for the breathtaking, phenomenal feeling of sliding in and out of this woman. This gorgeous, wonderful, sensual, bold woman. This sexual creature who wants me the same damn way I want her. Her hands curl tightly over my shoulders, and she grinds against me.

For a while, we're nothing but murmurs and sighs, moans and groans, and the slap of flesh against flesh. We become a carnal thing, a man and a woman hungry with desire, each consuming the other.

Then she grabs my face, grips me tight, and parts her lips. "Take me there," she says, her voice smoky and sexy, and pure vulnerability, too, as if she's spoken her greatest, deepest wish.

I push in deeper, reaching the edge of her, then I stop and stare into her eyes. I see everything that's seemingly struck me out of the blue, but now I'm sure has been there all along if I'd stopped to notice.

She's the woman for me.

She's the one I want.

I'm fucking my friend.

I'm screwing my roommate.

And more than that, I'm also making love to the woman I'm falling in love with.

But the more I think about the insanity and foolishness of me right now, the more I risk telling her everything. The more I'll ruin us.

Besides, right now I have one job. To take her there.

"I will, baby, I will," I say, then thread my fingers in her hair and bring my mouth to her ear as I fuck her hard and deep. She hooks her legs around my ass and pulls me tighter. I bury myself in her, fucking and thrusting until she screams so loudly that I know she's on the cusp.

Then, she tells me. Because that's what she does. She's an announcer.

I'm so close.

Keep fucking.

Just like that.

Like I'd stop.

She rocks up into me as if she's finding the perfect friction on my shaft, and soon she discovers it. She uncovers her pleasure, and an orgasm seems to blast through her. She trembles from head to toe. She shudders as she squeezes her eyes shut. "I'm coming," she whispers in the faintest, most desperate whisper.

Then a louder one. "Oh God, I'm coming."

Then an ear-splitting shout that rattles loose my own climax. It seizes me, crashing into me with the force of a storm, ripping through my body as I fuck her through my release, grunting her name, groaning barely coherent words. And as pleasure keeps rolling through me, I have to bite my tongue so I don't say anything more. So I don't tell her it's never been this good. And it's not just a scientific kind of good. It's a whole new level. One I fear I'm already becoming dangerously addicted to.

But I don't want to say that out loud yet, or ever. If I do, I could lose her, and that's a risk I just won't take.

Instead, we eat pizza.

CHAPTER TWENTY-TWO

I fold a slice and take another mouth-watering bite. After I chew, I roll my eyes in absolute appreciation of Josie's talents. "I was wrong all the other times. This is now the best thing you've ever made."

She laughs. "You said it's what you missed most in Africa."

"Oh, I definitely missed pizza with a ferocity."

"Say the word, and I'll make you a cherry pie, too," she says. When I give her a naughty wink, she holds up a hand. "I meant the kind with fruit in it."

"You do know there's no way for pie to sound anything but dirty?"

We're parked on the couch, half-dressed, after—no hyperbole—the best sex of my life. She fastened the apron again, and wears the cherry-patterned wrap and heels. She said she thought I'd get a kick out of her "post-sex" outfit. She was right. As for me, I'm in jeans.

"I do know that," she says, then stretches across the couch to ruffle my hair.

The gesture both warms my heart and makes me think. Josie's always been a toucher, so it's not out of place. But it feels so . . . couple-y. So boyfriend-girlfriend. There's a part of me that desperately wants that with her. That wants to just crack open my heart and tell her how I feel.

Because inside, I'm on cloud nine. I'm a happy motherfucker, just kicking back, eating pizza with the best girl I know. Our physical connection is mind-bogglingly good. We get along like two peas in a pod. She's been my friend forever. Hell, we're about to play a game of Scrabble before we go for round two.

But there's the rub.

Because all this floating on a cloud of complete and utter dirty, sexy, fantastic happiness is just smoke and mirrors. It's a trick designed flawlessly by the human body. Why, oh fucking why, does falling for someone have to be such a rush? Such a high?

But I know the answer.

There's a reason for the release of those endorphins. Chemicals are in our system so falling in love will make us procreate. This rampant contentment swirling inside me is all just basic survival-of-the-species shit. It's an illusion of brain chemistry.

And as long as I keep my head on straight, I can't be fooled by risky feelings.

Even though a part of me wants to throw caution to the wind, to listen to this hammering in my chest, to just say, "Hey, it's you and me, let's defy the odds." Fucking, eating pizza, and playing Scrabble.

Yeah, there's no need for anything more.

Until Josie clears her throat. "So . . ."

And that one word sucks up all the oxygen in the room.

All the happy, floaty, let's-get-drunk-and-screw vibe vanishes. It evaporates into the night. In one syllable, I know it's time to talk.

Though Josie and I can chat about anything, whatever comes after the "so" is the one thing I'm not ready to discuss. Because what's happening with us is fraught with too many complications. Screwing your roommate is like operating on a kidney, only you can't do it without harming a main artery. Too many systems are linked together—the home, the friendship, the sex, the rent. Even the utilities are part of our sex life.

Naturally, my next step is to try to defuse the bomb.

"By 'so', you mean the two-letter Scrabble word S-O, or the three-letter one that's an action performed by a seamstress?"

She laughs, shakes her head, and sets her hand on my thigh. "Chase," she says, and her tone is friendly but serious at the same damn time.

"Yeah?"

"We need to talk about what's going on. With us."

Like a steel rod has been implanted in my spine, I straighten and say roughly, "Okay."

Why does dread flood me at the mere prospect of this conversation?

Oh, right. Because the last woman I felt this way for had an affair while we were together. Ergo, relationships and me don't get along well. I open my heart, and it's stomped on. Add in the little, tiny, miniscule fact that falling for your friend means you're likely to lose that friend when the relationship goes belly up, and all I want to do is imitate a monk.

Well, just the vow-of-silence part. Not the other vows.

"You know how everything blends together for me?" she asks.

"Josie in a mixer," I answer.

A small smile is her response. "And this"—she points from her to me—"has the potential to make one big milkshake of emotions." The look in her eyes is fierce and resolute. "I know myself. You know me, too. You've seen how emotions all spill over. I don't try to compartmentalize. I'm no good at it. It's all here," she says, tapping her chest. "And with you and me, I can see this becoming the biggest milkshake of all. We're friends, we're roommates, and now we're lovers. I can't keep all the ingredients separated. Do you see what I mean?"

For the barest sliver of a second, I imagine we're going to skip the hard part. She'll say she's fallen for me, too, and let's just live like this forever and ever without a thing going wrong.

"Do you mean you like milkshakes?" I ask carefully, because I'm not sure if this is her preamble to telling me she's had the same goddamn epiphany I have and that we'll be the first pair of friends in the history of the universe not to fuck up the transition to the next "ship"—the one that goes with "relation."

There's a first time for everything, right?

She laughs lightly. "I do like milkshakes, Chase," she says and runs her fingers down my chest. "But you can't have them for every meal."

"The milkshake diet is completely physician approved," I deadpan.

But she's not in the mood to tease, or to eat sweets all day long, evidently. "What I mean is," she says, "I want us to be careful. I want us to have an understanding. I don't want to get my heart broken, and I don't want to hurt you, and most of all, I don't want to ruin our friendship."

And that's why I kept my mouth closed in the first place, and why the zipper on it will stay shut. Her words only cement the need for me to compartmentalize even if she can't. To keep love on one side, and sex on the other.

"Separate drawers," I say with a nod. I mime opening a bureau. "We need to keep this sex thing in a separate drawer"—then I close it—"and the friendship in another."

If we don't, we run the very real risk of losing the friendship.

She flashes a brief smile. "Yes. Don't you think that's the best way for us to stay in each other's lives?"

I nod because of course I've got to make sure she knows I'm not going to screw this up. I need her to know I can do as asked. "And you need me to help you keep the fact that I can make you come ridiculously hard in one drawer, and that I pay half the rent check in another?"

"And our awesome Scrabble teamwork in one more, please," she says, laughing. Then her chuckles quiet down. "It's not easy for me to keep everything on opposite sides. You have to know I'm completely and utterly turned on by you, that you absolutely get bonus points for being great in bed, and you're my dearest friend, and I think you're amazing." I can't help but grin at the compliments. "And I also can't bear the thought of losing you."

A life without Josie sounds like a living hell. "I don't want to lose you, either."

"That's why I need you to be the tough one. You need to be the doctor who rips off the Band-Aid eventually," she says with a rueful smile.

"Take advantage of the MD, why don't you," I grumble, jokingly.

But she's serious. "I don't want to be Adele. I don't want to be gone from your life." Her voice breaks, and this girl—God, she wears her emotions on her sleeve. She lets them out in the open for me to see. She's fearless and bold, not just in bed, but right here as she lays her heart on the line.

There's no tiptoeing around this topic. No doorbell ringing in the middle of a tough conversation, truncating it. Nope. We're not avoiding the issue—we're diving into the deep end as Josie opens her heart to me even more.

Everything she does makes me want her, in every way.

"That's why I think this is the only way to do this," she adds.

I swallow tightly, remembering the emptiness I felt when Adele moved on. I force myself to recall the hurt of losing someone I cared deeply for. Sure, the lonely nights sucked, but what ached more was the absence of a person I relied on. My friend. "I can't stand the thought of not being friends with you. We can't let that happen."

"I don't want that to happen, either," she says, her tone so earnest it hooks right into my chest. "But I also don't want to get fooled again like I did with Damien."

I give her a hard stare. "I'm not Damien. That guy surpassed acceptable levels of douchery by a million percent."

"I know, but it still hurt. I learned my lesson with him, and I want us to be completely clear from the get-go about what this can and can't be. We have to draw lines. We need to promise that whatever this sex thing is, we go back to being friends when we're done."

"Fine," I say, because that's what I want. To keep her.

"We just have to accept that we have crazy chemistry from living together, right?"

I nod. Maybe I even punctuate it with a wag of my tongue.

She laughs. "And we need to get that out of our system, right?"

I remind myself that compartmentalization is my special skill. I've honed it over the years. I've made it a goddamn practice. I take care of the body, and others handle the heart and mind. For once, Josie wants me to lean on my top talent —my ability to separate the physical from the emotional. She wants me to take the best possible care of her orgasms then send her on her way with regular friendship check-ups.

This ought to be easy.

This ought to be easy as pie.

"Josie, we are on the same page," I say, squaring my shoulders and giving her my best show of confidence. She doesn't need to know I'm stupidly falling for her. I'll apply the brakes and stop myself from falling further. This thing between us won't need to be more than a sweet little tryst with my sexy, gorgeous, daring, wild roommate.

All those strange sensations swarming my chest? Done. I'm giving them the boot. Tossing them out with the trash. *See you later, falling in love.*

Josie breathes a sigh of relief. "I'm so glad you feel the same way. I'd be so sad if you were out of my life."

I laugh and cup her cheek. "I'm not going anywhere. I'd never do anything to risk losing you. You're not just my friend. I hate to break it to Wyatt, but you're my best friend."

"You're mine, too." She beams. "It'll be our secret."

"Like 'Scotland's Burning.'"

"Look out, look out," she sings, and I join in our horrible duet.

When we're done massacring the song, I hold out a fist for knocking, keeping it all on the level. "We're roomies with benefits until we get it out of our system."

She knocks back, and we're all good now.

Only, I can't stop. I need to sell this to the judge and jury. I need to be thoroughly convincing so she doesn't know how close I was to spilling my guts. "And you should totally date," I add, all nonchalant.

She arches an eyebrow. "I'm not going to date while we're screwing."

"But when we're done," I add. Like the magnanimous, generous, wonderful friend I am. Who, evidently, likes to state the patently obvious.

"Okay," she says, hesitantly.

"When we're out of each other's systems," I add, and plaster on a smile, reminding her that we will be over eventually. We are a temporary fling. There's no point dwelling on how I felt earlier.

There's no point at all. Not even when we screw again that night on the couch. Not even when she wraps her arms around me and whispers my name. Not even when she tells me how good it is.

Nope. I don't let any of that affect me.

Not at all.

Not in the least.

I'm steel.

Even when she falls asleep in my arms again, curling up next to me and smelling like her, and like me, and like the best sex I've ever known. Because it was more than just sex.

Only . . . it can't be.

CHAPTER TWENTY-THREE
From the pages of Josie's Recipe Book

Josie's Chocolate Oh-No-You-Didn't-Do-That Milkshake Recipe

Ingredients

1 pint chocolate ice cream

Ideally some variety that is incredibly decadent and delicious, and will make you feel like you're falling . . . even though you're totally not, and you can't, and you won't.

1/4 cup milk

Milk is good for you! Milk makes for healthy bones! This recipe is clearly a health food.

Some ice

To numb your heart.

Dump all ingredients in a blender and blend on high until it's all one big milkshake of feelings, and emotions, and sex, and heartache, and friendship, and possibilities. Then, down the hatch.

Now, the next part of the recipe is the most essential. Once you've consumed the milkshake of your mixed-up, stirred-up, fused-and-confused feelings, brush your hands together, slap on a smile, and don't ever blend them again. Eat the ice cream *separately*, just like you're going to have that man.

That's all you can do to protect your heart. That's the only way to have him. Anything more and you might lose the best friend you've ever had.

CHAPTER TWENTY-FOUR

A few days later, after I treat a runner who collapsed from dehydration during his morning run in Central Park, the charge nurse marches over to me, a clipboard in hand.

"Dr. Summers, you're wanted," Sandy barks, her drill sergeant voice making me stand at attention.

I'm her soldier. "What have we got?"

I expect her to rattle off a litany of incoming trauma. Instead, she points her thumb in the direction of the lobby. "Pretty brunette in the waiting room asking for you."

My ears perk. My dick springs to attention. My heart leaps. Josie has stopped by. Maybe she brought me lunch. My stomach growls. Pavlovian organ. Come to think of it, my cock is, too, judging from the speed of its response to the words "pretty brunette."

Full-on salute in my scrubs. *Nice work, dick.*

It's no surprise, though, since the last few nights with Josie have been mind-blowing, and it's not only my mind that's been blown. But I haven't just been on the receiving end of the pleasure. Like Josie, I'm a taker and I'm also a giver. I've doled out multiple orgasms, and exponents of orgasms, too, administered in all sorts of ways.

She's voracious, and I've satisfied her appetite each and every time. Including with my tongue. When I first went down on her, once wasn't enough for either of us. I gave her a double like that, and she came even harder the second time.

The next morning, I found a bakery bag on the living room table with two chocolate chip cookies in it and a note that said: *Good things come in pairs.*

A day later, after a marathon session testing the sturdiness of our furniture, she left me a brownie, and the card attached read: *I think you burned this off last night. By the way, I'm super impressed with how sturdy our table is. Not to mention the wall.*

I can't wait to see why she's here at noon.

I thank Sandy then take off, striding through the corridor and past the nurse's desk. I push on the big, swinging doors that lead to the waiting room. A twenty-something dude in a hoodie hunches over in a chair, hacking. A muscular mom in yoga pants clutches a toddler in her arms. The kid's face is flushed, and he's shivering. Fever, I suspect. A handful of others wait, too, staring at phones or the TV hanging on the wall. We pride ourselves at Mercy on some of the shortest waits in the ER world, and judging from the markedly un-crowded lobby, we're doing okay in that pursuit.

But that also means it's easy to see Josie's not here. I de-flate. Yes, all the parts that were inflated.

"Hey, Dr. Summers."

I turn in the direction of a most decidedly masculine voice. The angular face is familiar. Sharp nose. Kind eyes. Blond hair. The light switches on. I smile and point at the guy. "Aquaman."

The man whose forehead doubled as a parking lot for a sex souvenir walks to me and extends a hand. He wears a sharp white dress shirt and expensive slacks. Funny, I didn't peg him for a wealthy businessman when he was in his Aquaman threads, but his duds today, from the cufflinks to the silk of his shirt, make it clear this man is rolling in it. You never know who likes to swing from the chandeliers.

I shake his hand, then turn to the aforementioned pretty brunette by his side.

"And the mermaid," I add, and she smiles and shakes my hand. A diamond ring sparkles on her finger. She's decked out in sharp clothes, too, with a full-on executive businesswoman look.

"I'm Cassidy," she says.

"Good to meet you. And good to see you again," I say to my former patient. "How's the chandelier abstinence program going?"

He smiles. His girlfriend does, too, her cheeks turning red. "We took your advice," he tells me. "The kitchen table is indeed a fine alternative."

"Excellent. And this," I say, pointing to his forehead. The tiniest of tiny scars is barely visible. "This looks good."

"I know," he says with a wide grin. "You can barely tell it's there."

His girlfriend sets a hand on his shoulder and gazes at him adoringly. "It's the perfect amount of rugged, sexy scar," she says sweetly, then dusts a kiss on his cheek. She turns to me. "And thank you, Doctor. You really did an amazing job stitching up Kevin. You can hardly tell."

"Excellent. That's my job. To make my work invisible."

"Invisible Man," Kevin says, like he just coined the moniker for a new superhero. He clears his throat. "We wanted to get you a little thank-you gift. For taking such good care of me. And for your suggestions. The table, but also another one you gave us. We took you up on it, and we hope you like it, too."

My eyebrows rise in curiosity.

Cassidy hands me a greeting-card-size envelope. I slide my thumb under the flap and open it. Inside is a white business card, along with a gift certificate for a cooking class. *Enticing appetizers and alluring desserts.*

I crack up, remembering our conversation on the exam table when I encouraged him to take a cooking class. "Well done, Aquaman. Well done."

Kevin smiles widely and holds his hands out in a sheepish shrug. "Doctor's orders. Far be it for me to defy them."

"You're a good man to follow them."

"And listen," he begins, adopting a more serious tone.

I tilt my head, waiting.

His blue eyes meet mine. "There's something else I need to thank you for."

I furrow my brow. "What's that?"

But when a siren blares, and the tell-tale sign of an incoming ambulance screeches outside, I say, "Sorry, but that's my cue to go."

We say a quick good-bye, and as I rush back into the ER, I make a hasty pit stop at the waiting room desk. A bleached blonde with tired eyes looks up at me. "Yes, Doctor?"

I nod at the sick toddler. "Make sure the kid gets seen as soon as you can, okay?"

She nods.

I head back to the madhouse, taking a quick glance at the gift along the way. It's a cooking class for two. I stuff it in my pocket, because we have a fifty-year-old man suffering from a heart attack coming in. This time, we save a life.

* * *

After a busy afternoon with no break in sight, I finish my shift and find a text from Wyatt.

In your hood. Grab a brew?

I text back with a yes, and we settle on a nearby location—Spencer and Charlotte's bar, The Lucky Spot. Spencer's behind the counter this time, and he tips his chin in greeting as we stroll in.

He pours some beers and places the glasses on the counter with a clang. "So a doctor and a carpenter walk into a bar…"

I roll my eyes. "Yeah? And what happens next? The bartender serves up a pale ale and a punchline?"

His green eyes study Wyatt and me. "Yes. Because want to know what happens when you cross a surgeon with a carpenter?"

"Oh, tell us, tell us," Wyatt says, mocking Spencer as he chimes in like an excited kid.

"I don't know . . . but I'd hate to see what they do with a saw," he says, then slaps his palm against the counter to punctuate his joke.

I groan. "Really?"

"That's the best you can do?" Wyatt asks.

Spencer points at my handyman friend. "I thought I nailed that one." Then he turns to me. "But not as well as Chase would have . . . killed it."

"Oh ha ha ha. I try to limit my kills," I say, lifting my glass to take a drink.

Spencer preens and blows on his nails. "All right, assholes. That'll be fifty dollars."

"You're cheap tonight," Wyatt remarks as he takes out his wallet and pretends to fish around for a big bill.

"Just kidding. Your money's no good here. For some reason, I let you two dickheads drink for free," he says, then heads to the end of his bar to take care of customers.

Wyatt and I shoot the breeze for a few minutes as we work on our pale ales, and then he levels me with an intense stare. "What's going on with Josie?"

I nearly spit out my drink.

The brother of the woman I'm trying desperately not to fall harder for laughs and claps my back. "Hard time holding your liquor?"

"Um, no, wrong pipe," I lie.

"Seriously, man. I've been thinking about our talk at Joe's Sticks. Is she doing okay on the whole dating scene?"

"Yeah. She's doing great," I say, fibbing outrageously and hating it.

"Dating any jackasses? Or have you weeded them all out?"

Briefly, my mind wanders back to the guy who made the gerbil comment, then to the idiot who tried to pry into her private life online, then to the one who started it all—Damien —by fooling my girl.

My girl.

I scrub a hand over my jaw. She's not mine. I can't think of her that way. I raise my glass. "You'll be glad to know I've safely kept her away from any and all jackasses."

I don't include myself in the jackass count. I'm not like those other guys. I'm not hurting Josie by sleeping with her like this. We have a temporary arrangement, an understanding, a roomies-with-benefits deal. If anything, I'm the one on the faster track to get hurt.

Wyatt clinks his glass to mine. "Good. I knew I could count on you to look out for my second-favorite person in the universe." Then sheepishly, in a lowered voice, he adds, "It's weird that I can't call Josie my favorite person anymore. She was for so long. For most of my life. But now that spot goes to the new Mrs. Hammer."

"Natalie's gotta be first, man."

Wyatt clasps my shoulder. "Good thing I've got you to make sure Josie's in good hands."

"Yeah, I'll definitely make sure of that," I say, looking away.

Because Josie is in my good hands, and I hope that's exactly where she's going to be in about an hour.

* * *

We text on the way home. She's on the express train. I'm on the local line. We laugh—over text—about how we're heading home at the same time.

Then, as I head up the steps of the station and onto the bustling sidewalk, her latest text sends a burst of excitement through me because I'll see her soon.

Josie: Want to do something crazy and, I dunno, walk the last few blocks together?

Chase: You are a wild thing.

Josie: I am. Especially when you learn what I have in store for you tonight.

A whistle rips through the warm early evening air, the kind a construction worker makes at a sexy woman. A familiar voice shouts at me, "Yo, Hot Stuff."

When I stop and turn around, Josie walks towards me, a little sway in her hips, a flirty grin on her pretty pink lips. She wears a short skirt with a swirly pattern on it, and a purple V-neck T-shirt. Her hair is cinched back in a ponytail, and her wrist is adorned with her silver bracelets.

She's so fucking hot. And beautiful. And bold.

I glance around, as if I'm looking for someone else. Then I stab my finger against my chest. "You talking to me?" I ask in my best movie gangster tone.

"Yeah, I'm talking to you with the nice ass."

I give it right back to her. "Turn around. Let me see yours."

She twirls once, then stops in front of me. "Hey, Doctor McHottie," she says in a softer but still sexy voice. She rises on tiptoe and gives me a peck on the cheek, and my heart races. Dumb organ. I need to remember that the heart's purpose is to pump blood, a body fluid that ferries nutrients and oxygen to cells. Its goal isn't to make me feel light-headed and dopily dizzy around her.

Even so, I clasp her jaw in my hand, and kiss her hard on the lips. If she's going to drop little whispery kisses on my face in public, I'm going to claim her naughty mouth with mine.

She moans lightly as I kiss her, and I swallow that sound. When I break the kiss, a soft sigh escapes her lips. I roam my eyes over her. As I catalogue her ridiculously cute outfit, an abhorrent thought pops into my brain. "Were you on a date after work?"

A tornado of jealousy sweeps through me. But I have no right to feel envious, since she's not mine. I better revise my jackass tally since I clearly belong on it now.

She shakes her head. "No. I went to dinner with Lily. To a little sandwich shop on the East Side," she says, as we walk through the New York night toward our building.

"How is she?"

Josie smiles. "She's finally giving Rob the boot. I hate to say it, but I'm so glad. He was no good for her." She hooks her arm through mine, and I tamp down a smile because right now we seem like a hell of a lot more than two roomies heading home together.

I flash back to Wyatt's comments about dates, to Josie's re-marks about not dating, and to the gift certificate I shoved out of my mind all day. "Is there any chance you'd want to take an Enticing Appetizers and Alluring Desserts class with me?"

My voice sounds dry as I ask the question, as if I've never asked a girl out before. As I wait, the thumping in my chest has the audacity to reappear. I hope she'll say yes.

She quirks up one eyebrow. "The sensual cooking class?"

I blink. "That's what it is? I just thought it was a fun desserts class, and I know you like to try those out."

She nods. "I've heard it's amazing."

"Want to go?"

She nods eagerly. "I'd love to."

Guess that means I have a date with Josie now.

There's a spring in my step as we reach the building. But I remind myself it's not a date. She's just a friend. She's just a girl I live with.

When the elevator door closes I'm ready to pounce on her. Cage her in my arms. Kiss the hell out of her. But a weather-worn woman with silver streaks in her hair follows us in, her husband behind her.

I raise my chin, recognizing them as fellow residents in this building. "Hey there. How's your evening?"

She tuts and shakes her head. "It was a good one, until I checked the mailbox." She holds a stack of envelopes in her hand. "I've always detested the mail. Bills, bills, bills."

Her husband nods sagely.

"Mail can have a way of bringing you down," Josie chimes in. "Unless someone sends cookies, money, or candy."

The woman laughs. "Now, that would be a good mail day."

They exit on the fifth floor. When the elevator slows at our floor, I return to Josie's last text. "What did you have in store for me tonight?"

A flirty look is her answer as she exits and leaves me with this enticing command: "Come find me in ten minutes and you'll see."

CHAPTER TWENTY-FIVE

A lustful kind of anticipation camps out in my body. This is the adult equivalent of waiting for Santa Claus. And I was one hell of a fan of the jolly man in red. But right now, as I knock back a glass of Scotch in the kitchen and check the time, I'm confident that whatever is waiting for me under the tree that is Josie's bedroom will be better than any bike, *Star Wars* toy, or game of Operation I've ever received.

And I did love Operation.

But I love sex way more.

Let me amend that. I love sex with Josie way more than any gift. More than nearly anything.

The sound of a slow, sexy song drifts through the apartment. I close my eyes, listening. It's low and seductive, and I can't make out the words from here, but I recognize an invitation when I hear one.

I finish the amber liquid, set the glass on the counter, and follow the sound of the honey-voiced singer.

Our place is small. It doesn't take me long to reach Josie's room. The music grows louder. Sounds like one of those female crooners with voices that ooze sex appeal. The words and lyrics do the same, too. Joss Stone maybe, singing about the higher you take her.

The door is ajar. A sliver of light shines into the hall. I rap lightly.

"Come in." Her voice is smoky, like this song.

When I push open the door all the breath rushes out of my lungs. "Jesus fucking Christ," I groan, as my cock thickens.

Josie rests on top of the white covers, her brown and pink hair fanned out on a pillow. She wears pink lace panties and one of those bras that cover only half her miraculous tits. Demi-something, I think it's called.

Actually, I don't give a shit what her lingerie is named.

I'm renaming this ensemble the most arousing thing a woman has ever worn. Though, what makes the sight such an immense turn-on is the location of Josie's hands.

One cups her right breast, kneading.

The other? Dear God in heaven. The other hand plays between her legs. Her busy fingers stroke the wet panel of her panties.

My dirty reel has come to life. She meets my eyes, and the glint in them beckons me.

I swallow dryly. My throat is parched, and I grab the tail of my shirt, tug it over my head, then unzip my jeans in a flash. I set a new record for undressing when my briefs come off a nanosecond later.

"You," I rasp out, as I get on the bed at her feet. "You're so fucking sexy we're going to need a new word for it."

She smiles at me, her finger rubbing the outline of her swollen clit. Breathily, she asks, "Is this the kind you like to watch?"

I set my hands on her knees, opening her legs more as I stare at the gorgeous, erotic, beautiful sight in front of me. My girl in pink, her panties wet, touching herself because she can't help it.

I shake my head. "I don't *like* this. I fucking *love* it, Josie."

Kneeling, I take my throbbing cock in my hand, running my palm down the length.

Her hips shoot up. "Oh God, that's so hot," she moans.

"Yeah?" I do it again, stroking my dick as she watches me.

"That's what I was picturing before you walked in." Her fingers move faster. I can't look away from her. Not that I would. I'm not insane. I am, however, insanely aroused because she's so fucking wet. She's become my greatest fantasy. "You jerking off on me," she says.

Jesus Christ.

I was wrong.

This is greater than my hottest fantasy.

Because she's not just getting off—she's getting off to *me*.

"Take these off now." Reaching for her panties, I tug them down her hips, along her luscious thighs, and over her ankles. Her fingers immediately return to her pussy, but I shake my head.

"I want you naked. Bra, too," I tell her, and as she unhooks it, I press my hands to her thighs and part her legs farther.

My dick is so hard right now, it's fucking aching for attention, but *this*—her bare pussy is the stuff dirty dreams are made of. She's slick and wet, and so wildly turned on by thoughts of *me*.

I'm floored—fucking floored—by the utter dirty perfection of this woman.

Now that her glorious tits are freed and she's as naked as I am, I tip my chin in the direction of her pussy. "Now resume doing the sexiest fucking thing I've ever seen."

Her nimble fingers return to her wet center, and the second she touches herself, she moans. Lifting her hips, she seeks out her own pleasure. Her eyes float shut again as she strokes all that delicious wetness.

"Oh God," she murmurs, and that sound is like a bolt of heat straight to my dick. Wrapping a fist around my hard-on, I stroke.

"This is how we were the other week," I say as I move my hand up and down my erection. "Jerking off to each other."

She opens her eyes, her green irises hazy with lust. "I thought about you so many times, Chase," she moans as she rubs her sweet little clit with abandon.

"Did I make you come every time?"

She nods as she rocks her hips. "Every time. All the time. You fucked me so many times." Her pace quickens and her breathing turns erratic.

"Josie," I say on an upstroke that sends a hot tremor through me. "Fuck yourself with your fingers."

Her eyes widen, and then her fingers get to work. She slides one inside her pussy, then another, all while she works the delicious rise of her clit with her thumb.

And hell, if the sight in front of me isn't enough for me to come right now, I don't know what is. But I grit my teeth and call off the dogs, because I'm not firing before she does.

I need to watch every second of the hottest X-rated video I've ever seen. I won't miss a frame.

Her other hand spears into her hair, and she turns her head to the side, her lips parting, her panting loud. Then it becomes a chorus of *oh God* and *oh God, I'm so close.*

And she fucks herself.

With abandon.

With intensity.

With a wild need to come.

I see it in her features, in the torment on her face as she nears the edge, in the mad speed of her fingers as she thrusts in and out, in her thumb as she strokes and strokes and strokes until she hits that high note.

She calls out a last *oh God*, and her hips rise up.

And then she trembles.

Like a full-body shudder. I swear, I can see her orgasm move through her. It's the most beautiful thing I've ever witnessed—the way Josie comes. She doesn't hold back. Not her mouth, not her body, nothing. "Oh my God, oh my God, fuck me."

I don't mind if I do.

My own release isn't far off, but I don't slide into her since I don't have a condom close enough. Instead, I climb up her, straddling her waist as I jerk my cock harder.

Pleasure rattles through me and I groan.

She blinks open her eyes and seems to register where I am. She pushes her breasts together, and that's all I need to know.

I slide in and fuck her tits, bracing my palm on the pillow by her face.

Now this? This is a whole new realm of heaven. My dick is in my favorite place, and I'm seconds from coming. She pushes her tits even tighter, creating a warm tunnel for my shaft. On an upstroke, Josie sticks out her tongue and flicks the head of my cock.

It feels magnificent.

And it flips the switch.

"Gonna come," I grunt, and with a loud groan I shoot jets over her chest. I shudder, my shoulders shaking as my climax thunders through me.

"Holy fucking shit," I mutter. Because it was so fucking good.

Because of her.

When I come down from my high, I reach over to her nightstand and grab some tissues. "Let me clean this."

I wipe me off her chest as she murmurs, "I liked it, though."

"Yeah? Were you going to wear my come all night?"

She laughs lightly and shrugs. "I like it when you come on me."

I stand and toss the tissues in a trash can, then return to her, gathering her in my arms. "You do?"

She nods and tilts her chin up, meeting my eyes. "It's my favorite thing—making you come," she says softly, then runs a finger down my chest. Her touch is electric, and even though I just finished, I'm getting hard again. "I like when you come inside me." Her fingers trail down my pecs. "And in my mouth." Then to my abs. "And on my body." Over my hip. "I just love it when it feels good for you."

I'm so stunned by the sheer sensuality of her words and by the gorgeous honesty in them that I barely know what to say. Instead, I drop my mouth to hers and kiss her softly, then harder still, because the taste of her lights me up, and it shuts my mouth.

That way, I won't slip and say the words she doesn't want to hear. Words that clog my throat and fight to come out. Words that I have to shove back down because they'd reveal everything.

I barely understand how she can say something so raw and sexual to me, and not only does it turn me on beyond any and all reason, but it also hooks into my heart and makes me fall harder for her.

When she breaks the kiss, I wriggle my eyebrows. "I love it when you come, too. So let's make that happen."

I move down her body, kissing her beautiful breasts, her soft waist, the curve of her hips, then I bury my face between her legs, licking her until she comes again. My name is on her lips with every shudder, every tremble, every cry.

And it kills me.

It kills me how much I want her in every way.

And later, when I put her on her hands and knees and fuck her until she groans, I groan, and the bed groans, I revise my earlier sentiment about her chest being my favorite place.

She is my favorite place.

And I'm ridiculously glad I have a date with her, even though I doubt it'll be the first of many, like I want.

The clock ticks on this thing between us. The more we spend nights in bed, the harder it'll be to carry on as just friends when this ends.

CHAPTER TWENTY-SIX

If I thought Josie was into playing mood music the other night, she's got nothing on Ivory.

The teacher of the sensual cooking class pipes in a constant stream of Sade at the cooking school in Soho on a Friday night.

Oh, and she's also arranged scented candles around the room. I suspect she hopes we're all going to get it on right here on the kitchen counter after we prep the chocolate-covered strawberries.

Josie and I aren't the only ones taking the Enticing Appetizers and Alluring Desserts class, but I think we might be the only couple that's barely a couple. Or the only pair not quite taking this class as seriously as all the others.

There's an older couple here, in their sixties maybe. The man has his paws all over his woman. I'm not opposed to PDA in theory, but I'm not all that interested in seeing him grope her ass incessantly. But it's nice that they dig each other. A younger couple is here, and the woman is pregnant. They might be trying to get pregnant while pregnant tonight, if such a thing were possible, judging from how many times he kisses her as they chop vegetables. Two men are here, too, and they're quite touchy-feely as well.

Fine, it's a sensual cooking class, but it's a bit like we're on an episode of *Couples Retreat—Watch The Modern Man and Woman Mate. Or Man and Man. Or Woman and Woman.*

And look, I'm all for getting it on with Josie as much as possible. Just not in a class. Tonight, she wears a summery dress along with her cherry-patterned apron, and surprise, surprise, it makes me think of the first time we made—

Screwed, I mean.

That's all it was, and she looks completely screwable in her apron, as she mixes melted chocolate in a glass bowl at the wooden counter.

We've already cooked a pepper dish, while Ivory, in her slinky red dress, opined on how the heat in peppers stimulates blood, endorphins, and, you got it, erections. Considering I'm hard nearly all the time around Josie, I don't need peppers to serve as my Viagra. But peppers are tasty, so we nibbled on that enticing appetizer.

Oysters came next, and Ivory watched over us, encouraging Josie to feed them to me. I declined. "You should try them. They make you virile," Ivory said.

"Already there," I told her.

She moved on to another couple, and I whispered to Josie, "Can't stand oysters."

She crinkled her nose. "I can't either, so that was the right answer on the Roommate Compatibility test."

Next, our teacher waxed on about asparagus and bananas, citing both the stimulants contained in them, but also how their shapes served as foreplay.

Everyone nodded sagely, like Ivory was sharing some new-found wisdom. But no one seemed able to utter the reason why their shape might be a turn-on.

"You mean because they're phallic?" Josie asked, as if she were just learning this fact.

"Yes," Ivory said, stroking a banana. "See?"

"Oh, I get it now," Josie said.

When the teacher turned around, Josie opened her mouth wide like she was about to fellate the fruit. That made my night.

Yeah, maybe we're goofballs. Maybe we're irreverent. Maybe this class isn't exactly for us. It's a bit too serious, but we're having fun in our own way.

Especially now that it's dessert time.

"Chocolate is the ultimate aphrodisiac," Ivory says, wandering around the room like a dance instructor. Her dark hair is braided down her back. She stops at a hipster couple—a guy with black glasses and a goatee, who slices strawberries next to a woman with a pixie cut. Ivory places one hand on his shoulder, the other on hers. "Chocolate is delicious, but that's not the only reason it's an aphrodisiac. Do you know why it is?"

The woman clears her throat. "They say it makes you feel like you're falling in love?"

Ivory nods and holds up a finger. "They do say that. But why? Why does chocolate make you feel like you're in love?"

Josie steals a glance at me, and for a second I think it's because of the topic. That she can read it in my eyes, or that she's checking to see if I might feel that way. Nerves crawl up my throat, but when Josie nudges me, it's clear she's just having fun. "I know the scientist in you is dying to answer," she says under her breath.

She's not wrong. I rocked at school. Hell, I didn't skip two grades for nothing. I loved taking tests, loved answering questions, and loved getting the answers right. Part of me wants to shout, "It's chemistry."

But Ivory keeps going. "Chocolate is an aphrodisiac because it melts on the tongue, and because it improves circulation. But most importantly, it strengthens the heart." She stops in the middle of the room and surveys her cooking students at each station. "And do you know what a strong heart does?"

I. Can't. Resist.

I speak up. "A strong heart beats one hundred thousand times a day and pumps about two thousand gallons of blood through the circulatory system to sustain life. When the heart is strong, you can do everything better, faster, and longer." Ivory watches me with wide eyes. "That also means a strong heart improves endurance." I square my shoulders. "Including between the sheets."

Out of the corner of my eye, I notice Josie's lips twitching. Her hand covers her mouth. Then a small laugh slips past her fingers.

"Very good," Ivory says with a nod. "And you see, class, chocolate is good for the heart because it helps ensure you can last all night long."

Josie grabs my arm and digs her nails in, no doubt so she doesn't crack up.

"And now let us enjoy the stimulant," Ivory says, holding her arms out wide, as if she's our Sherpa guiding us up the mountain of sexual exploration. "Let us dip the strawberries in the chocolate and feed them to our partners."

Josie turns to me, a naughty little grin on her face as she holds a strawberry and whispers, "Open wide."

I do, flicking my tongue out, letting her know what I want to be eating.

My date brings a chocolate-covered strawberry to my tongue. It's tasty, and I finish it quickly. Then I notice everyone else is moving in slow motion, taking their time with the berries, rolling them around on their tongues, dusting kisses on their partners' mouth.

Make no mistake—I would love to be kissing Josie right now. But in private. Not on display. I lower my voice. "I feel like we're in a Lamaze class, and we're the only ones not totally into it."

She laughs. "Same here. Also, I already knew all this stuff about the food. Sort of like you and the heart," she says, tapping mine.

Her hand on me feels good. It reminds me where I want to be.

Not here.

Evidently, she feels the same because she mouths, "Want to make a run for it?"

I lunge as if I'm about to take off in a race. Josie shakes her head, then dips her hand in her purse, fiddles around with something, and soon my phone bleeps loudly from my pocket.

Josie turns her expression to one of worry. "Oh my God, is that the hospital?" she says in a stage whisper.

I slide into my role. "It must be," I say heavily. "I'm on call tonight."

I grab my phone, swipe my thumb across the screen, and bring it to my ear, answering it professionally. I pretend to listen to instructions. When the imaginary answering service is through, I say, "I'll be right there. Make sure to stabilize the patient and start an IV drip."

All eyes in the room snap to me. "I'll be there in ten minutes." For Josie's amusement, I add in a deeply ominous tone, "And whatever you do, Bob, don't lose the patient."

Dun. Dun. Dun.

I end the call, and Ivory points to the door. "Go! Godspeed."

We take off into the Soho night, laughing as we make our great escape from the too touchy-feely cooking lesson.

"What a strange class," Josie says as we head to the subway. "Funny, because I heard so many raves about it."

"I get why it's fun, but maybe it's not for us. To each his or her own, I suppose. The guy who recommended it liked to hang on chandeliers."

We stop at the crosswalk, waiting for the light. She looks up at the faint stars in the sky, as if she's thinking. "The whole idea of aphrodisiacs or sensual food is cool, but maybe it's not the food that's sensual." She meets my eyes. "Maybe it's the person. Maybe it's just who you're with, and it's not about the candlelight, or the music, or the way you feed someone."

I drop my hand to her shoulder and serve up the full truth. "Josie, you could eat tuna fish and I'd still be turned on."

She brings a hand to her chest and bats her eyes. "I think that's the sexiest thing you've ever said to me."

Then we go underground.

CHAPTER TWENTY-SEVEN

Let me be perfectly clear. The subway is not an aphrodisiac. But Josie is.

The whole ride uptown, we talk. About the class. About food. About what might happen on the next season of *Vice Principals*. She slides her hand into my hair and absently plays with the ends as we talk.

And this, right here, on the noisy, dirty, grimy subway is the true turn-on. Me and my girl, heading home. As the train slaloms past Fourteenth Street, she drops her hand and reaches for mine.

My breath hitches as she squeezes my fingers. That's all it takes. Her holding my hand. I let my head fall back, hitting the window behind us.

"Are you okay?" she asks.

"I'm perfect."

Perfectly ruined for anyone else.

I take our joined hands and press a kiss to her knuckles, wondering what the hell I'm supposed to do about the fact that she's not out of my system. Not even close. Not one single bit.

She rests her head on my shoulder.

We aren't hand-holders. We aren't daters. We aren't affectionate.

At least, not in public.

And in private, we're usually naked.

But tonight on the train, she's been playing with my hair, snuggling against me, looping her fingers through mine. It doesn't take a genius to figure out this is couple behavior, and it's coming from a woman who made it crystal clear she wanted to be roomies-with-benefits only. Has something changed for her?

A wild idea descends on me. Could she want . . .

No. I can't let myself think that. It's crazy, and beyond the realm of expected outcomes.

Even so, my heart skips a beat. My skin heats up. And something like hope makes landfall in my chest. It feels like a wild, crazy possibility, but it's one I desperately want right now—to simply slide from this phase to the next one without a hitch. To be the exception. To pull this whole crazy thing off.

I hold that thought close as we walk home.

When we reach our building, the mustached doorman gives a quick hello, then points to the elevators. "The main elevator is out of commission. We're having some work done to it. The service elevator is working, but it's a bit slow. It should return to the lobby in a few minutes."

"We'll take the stairs," Josie says to him with a smile. "We have strong hearts and good endurance."

He adjusts his green blazer. "Oh, and Ms. Hammer. The postman delivered something for you. Would you like me to get it from the mail storage room?"

She shakes her head. "I'll grab it tomorrow. I'm sure it's the rolling pin I ordered."

We head to the stairwell, and I open the door, letting her go ahead of me.

As she walks, I enjoy the view of her legs, her ass, her skirt. At the first landing, I grab her hand and pull her back, her chest pressed to me. "You're the enticing appetizer."

She sighs sexily and brings her hands to my chest. "So are you."

Her lips part, and my God, what the fuck am I supposed to do?

But kiss her.

And hold her.

And have her.

And want her.

It's a slow, sensual kiss at first. A tease. The start of something. And when she murmurs against my mouth, all bets are off. I band my arm around her waist and tug her close, sealing her body to mine. "I'm seriously considering fucking you in the stairwell," I tell her.

She lowers her hand to the front of my jeans, rubbing the outline of my cock. "Love that idea. But I want to be naked with you."

I groan and smack her ass. "Upstairs," I growl. "As fast as you can. Get that dress off and then get on me."

"Yes, sir."

She scurries up the next set of stairs, then the next. When we near the fourth floor, she sneaks a glance back. "Peekaboo," she says, then lifts up the back of her skirt, flashing me her panties.

Her red lace, see-through panties.

Heat roars through me, and instinct takes over. I reach for her, and when my shoe hits the landing, the ankle rolls out, and my foot turns in.

An instant, searing pain rips along my right calf and straight into my ankle, a shot of misery.

"Fuck," I curse, as my ankle yelps.

Josie flies down the steps in a flurry. "Oh no. Are you okay?"

I wince. "Yeah," I bite out, bending over to grip my ankle.

Her hand runs up my back, a reassuring pat. "Babe, are you okay? You're worrying me."

"Fine," I mumble.

I straighten, because I can't be that guy. The helpless guy.

"Let me help you," she says, moving to my side and draping her arm around me.

"I'm fine."

"You're not. Let me help you." Her voice is firm.

"I swear I'm okay."

"Stop being such a macho man."

She wins the battle and walks with me the rest of the way up the stairs as I try not to limp. "It was my butt's fault," she says, contrition in her tone. "My cheeks distracted you."

I dart a hand down to squeeze one. "Your butt is worth a twisted ankle."

When we reach the apartment, the pain shoots through me once more, and I pretty much limp inside, Josie holding open the door.

"Go sit," she directs, pointing. "On the diddle couch."

I do, plopping down on the soft cushions. I'm grateful to be surrounded by all these pillows. I lift my right ankle onto the coffee table as Josie sets her hands on my shoulders. "Tell me what you need. Ice, I presume?"

I nod. "Ice and ibuprofen, too. And elevation. But I took care of that part."

She marches to the bathroom and returns quickly with two pills and a cup of water. I down the ibuprofen. She rounds the corner into the kitchen and reappears seconds later with a hand towel and an ice pack. She wraps the towel over the pack, takes off my shoes and socks, and pushes up the bottom of my pant leg. She parks herself on the table and presses the pack gently to my ankle.

"Ouch! It's freezing."

She rolls her eyes. "It's supposed to be frozen. It's ice."

"It's so cold."

"Has anyone ever told you that you're a terrible patient?"

I frown. "I try to never be the patient."

A soft smile plays on her face. "But this time, you have a nurse who offers a special brand of TLC."

And my foot isn't cold anymore. In fact, it barely hurts at all when Josie rests the ice on my foot, cuddles up by my side, and kisses the hell out of me.

Ten minutes later, my foot is frozen, but everything else is on fire.

"You going to be okay?" she asks.

"I'll live," I say with a pout. There's one good thing about twisted ankles—the recovery time is quick. There's a bigger problem, though, in my pants. I cast my gaze to my hard-on. "But can you do anything about this new issue you've created?"

A grin spreads on her face. "That is my special nursing talent," she says, standing and stripping. With each shred of clothing that comes off, I'm harder and more aroused. How that's possible, I don't know. But that's the Josie effect. She does this to me, and I help her along by unzipping my jeans and pushing them to my knees.

In her naked glory, she grabs a condom from the table and straddles me. I brush strands of pink hair from her face. "Your pink is fading," I say, as I run a finger over her locks.

"I need to touch it up. I'll do it tomorrow morning, since I'm not working. Takes me a little while since I have to focus on putting the color in so I don't get it all over my neck," she says as she opens the condom wrapper.

"Do you want me to help? I have steady hands."

"You'd do that?"

"Of course," I say, wishing I could add the full truth. *I'd do anything for you.*

She drops a kiss to my lips then rolls the condom onto my dick. So much for the hair talk. All I care about now is *this*. She lowers herself onto me, and her wet, warm pussy hugs my cock. We groan in unison. Electricity rushes through me. Pleasure spreads to every damn molecule. I grip her hips. "Jesus, Josie."

She rises up on my dick, then back down. "I know, right? It's so good." Her voice sounds as if it's breaking.

I cup her cheeks as she rides me. "What am I going to do with you?"

She shakes her head, like she barely knows the answer either.

"You're so fucking good to me," I say, then crush her lips to mine.

I don't know how to do this. Not when she owns me, not when she takes care of me, and not when she fucking wins my heart over and over.

I can't stop feeling this way. I can't stop falling. I'm so fucking in love with her, it hurts. I want to be the one who wants her, and be the one she wants, just like she asked for.

"One guy who wants me the way I want him."

You have him, I want to say. He's right fucking here.

She breaks our kiss as she rides me harder and wilder, and it's spectacular watching her chase her pleasure. I drop my hand to her legs, rubbing her clit as she fucks me until she shudders and then breaks apart.

Her face falls next to mine, cheek to cheek, her mouth near my ear. "I don't know how to stop."

Hell if I know how, either.

* * *

Later, when we're in bed, and I reassure her for the tenth time that her medicine worked and my ankle's fine, she sets her hand on my shoulder. "Did you enjoy our date?"

That last word makes my breath catch. Her voice is nervous, like she truly hopes I'll say yes.

"Loved it," I say as I run my fingers through her hair.

"Even the kooky teacher and the class that totally wasn't our style?"

I nod. "Even that."

"It was perfect for us," she says softly, snuggling closer.

Our. Date. Us.

That well of hope? It springs up again. This is the turning point. This is when she says she's all in. This is us without a hitch.

She sighs and cuddles up against me. "I wish it could be like this."

I tense. Because that doesn't sound like *all in*. "Like what?" I ask carefully.

"Like tonight. Perfect. Even with your ankle."

"But it can't be?"

She looks up and meets my eyes. "I don't want to lose you. You know that."

I nod, afraid if I speak I'll ruin what we have.

Or maybe she will, given her next words. "Chase," she says slowly, her voice sad. "What happens when this ends?"

My chest aches. My heart stings. "What do you mean?" I choke out.

She waves in the direction of my wall, my room, and draws a deep breath like it fuels her. "Do you just go back to your bed? To your room?"

"I don't know," I say, each word like a stone in my mouth.

"I don't want this to stop," she says, and I want to grab her, hold her, tell her it doesn't have to. "But it has to, right?"

Her voice wobbles, like she's on the cusp of tears. For a second, hope tries to jostle its way past the pragmatic reality that friends who dally too far into benefits are doomed. Because it sounds like she doesn't want this to end, either. Like she's looking for the loophole, too.

But I'm not sure it exists.

In medicine, there are risks, there are side effects. You have to weigh them and decide if the treatment is worth the cure. Taking the leap with Josie, telling her I'm crazy in love with her, isn't like popping some Advil for my ankle. It's jacking up my whole body with steroids that could do serious damage down the line.

"Right?" she asks again, like she needs me to be the one to keep the ingredients separate.

I flash back to her worries and her words the first night we slept together.

"I need you to be the tough one. You need to be the doctor who rips off the Band-Aid eventually."

I look into her eyes. She's waiting for my answer. She needs me to be strong. *Fuck.* I don't want to play that role with her.

But if we're going to pull this off— the return to Friend-shipland—I've got to.

I push past the lump in my throat. "Right."

She sighs, and the sound is both wistful and horribly pained. "We'll be like a cake that bakes too long. You've got to know when to take it out of the oven or it'll burn."

"I don't want to burn," I say.

But I fear I already have.

CHAPTER TWENTY-EIGHT

From the pages of Josie's Recipe Book

An Apple a Day

Ingredients

Any Kind of Apple

1. Take an Apple.

2. Eat it.

3. Hope to hell it works, even though there's a part of you that doesn't want it to work at all. Not one bit. Not in the least.

4. You know what an apple a day does.

CHAPTER TWENTY-NINE

She's sound asleep, the sheet having slipped down to her waist. Her features are soft in the dark-blue light of the early hour. Her brown hair spills over her pillow, and her breathing is slow and even.

The clock flashes 5:30, and it's not just a warning that it's time for me to leave. It's a reminder that we're another moment closer to the end. Josie and I might not have an official expiration date, but we're as good as fully cooked.

Maybe one more night. Maybe one more time. Last night, she made it clear that the timer buzzes any minute.

I heave a sigh as I pull on work-out shorts and a T-shirt. Turning away from her, I head to the bathroom and brush my teeth.

I grab my bike shoes and pad quietly across the floor, favoring my right foot. I lied last night. My ankle did hurt. It still does, but I'm going to ride with Max this morning anyway. I close the door with a soft whoosh so I won't wake her up.

In the hallway, I put on my shoes. I snag my bike from the basement and dart downtown, the early-morning cabs and buses keeping me company on the road, along with my thoughts.

I wish there were other options.

But this—having her in every way—is the kind of procedure that reeks of malpractice. It's fraught with too many known risks that can lead to a negative outcome, including injury or death.

I try to weigh the choices like I'd evaluate such a complicated treatment.

On the one hand, I could tell her how I feel. But that's a surgical procedure with a great likelihood of morbidity. What if telling her freaked her out? Worried her? Made her kick me out of the apartment and say, *Sorry bud, you're not the full package I want?* We might as well kill the friendship on the operating table.

On the other hand, we could apply the brakes, preserve the friendship, and save the patient—our friendship.

That's the safest choice.

The only other option is so crazy, so ridiculous, I can't even take it seriously. It's the one where I tell her how I feel, and miraculously, she wants the same thing. We'd skip merrily down the street into la-la-happy-fucking-forever-and-ever land.

I scoff at that scenario as I slow at a light.

We have a name for that in the ER. It's the hallelujah scenario. It's the outcome so wonderfully unexpected in the face of outrageously bad odds that patients and families deem it a miracle.

You can't count on miracles. You can't practice for them. And you certainly can't bet something as critical as a life on them.

When I reach Max's building and wheel up to the lobby door, a heaviness descends upon my bones. There's only one procedure to perform. Josie and I will have to return to the way we were, like we'd planned. We'll remain the best of friends, and these last few weeks will simply be a fun little blip. We'll look back on this time and laugh about the days when we were roomies-with-bennies.

Max strolls out of the lobby, pushing his bike. He lifts his chin. "Hey."

"Hey."

"Ready?"

"I'm ready."

We ride along our usual route as the sun rises. But I'm off my game. That heaviness has spread through my body. It weighs me down. It slows me. I'm as sluggish as I've ever been.

From several bike-lengths ahead, Max glances back and shouts, "C'mon, man. Catch up."

It's not an admonishment—it's an encouragement. My brother knows me. He knows speed is my asset. This morning, though? My legs are lead.

I can't do it.

Max slows and stops. "What's going on?"

I roll up beside him on the path. "Nothing."

He shakes his head then points to a nearby bench. We wheel over to it, unsnap our helmets, and park our asses, resting our bikes on the grass.

"Something's going on."

I drop my head into my hands. I can't fucking hold this in a second longer. "I'm in love with Josie, but I can't be."

For the briefest moment, my body feels light. I said it out loud. I voiced it to another person.

When I raise my face, I half expect my brother to laugh at me. But I know better. That's not Max's style.

"Love sucks." He exhales heavily and meets my eyes. "Does she feel the same?"

I shrug. "I don't know. But it doesn't matter. She said we need to stop."

Max holds up his hands in a *T*. "Whoa. Stop what?"

And so I tell him the CliffsNotes version.

"Chase," he says with a sigh that contains all the older brother wisdom in the world.

"I know."

He shakes his head. "She's gonna break your heart, man."

I snap my gaze to him. "What?" I heard him, I just refuse to believe Josie would do that.

"Look at you. You're a mess. She's going to hurt you. Like that—"

I cut him off before he can say "Adele." I don't feel the need to defend my ex, but I can't bear to have her name breathed near Josie's. "It's not the same."

"I know, but fuck." He drags a hand through his hair, heaving a sigh. "I hate seeing you so worked up over a woman."

"She's not just any woman."

"I get that." He stares me down. His dark eyes have always felt like laser beams. "She's your roommate, and your best friend, and your lover, and you want her to be your girl-friend." He takes a beat and shakes his head as if he's frustrated with the situation. "But she's told you that can't happen, and you're setting yourself up for a world of hurt."

He's right. Hell, I know he's right. And the dread that floods every corner of my body is the proof of how right he is. But still, some faint hope nags at me. "You sure?"

"Look, there's probably some school of thought that would tell you to man up and let her know how you feel. And hey, maybe you should. Lord knows, I don't have the track record to be any sort of relationship expert." He scrubs a hand over his jaw. "But, Chase . . . this? This is a precarious house of cards." He makes a flicking motion with his finger, knocking over the imaginary structure. "I just don't see how you can pull off this trick without everything tumbling down. She's not some nurse you're hot for who works the same shift. She's not a chick you met online, or a babe you hooked up with at a car show."

I laugh for a second because that last is his weakness, not mine. "I thought you were cutting back on that?"

He makes a scout's honor sign. "I'm on the wagon." He grips my shoulder. "Anyway, the point is . . . she's Josie," he says, with an intensity that matches how I feel for her. "You've had a thing for her for about . . . forever. Everyone knew it but you."

I arch an eyebrow. "Everyone?"

"Dude, it's patently obvious. You flirt with her constantly. Your face lights up when she comes in the room. You smile like an idiot when you talk about her."

I sneer. "Shut up. I do not."

"You do, too."

I scowl, proving just how much I'm not a love-struck fool.

"That's why I don't see how even you can pull this off," he says. "If anyone can manage balancing acts and feats of strength, it's my little brother. But this isn't just pushing your body to finish a race, or to handle a thirty-six-hour shift without a yawn. This isn't even skipping two grades in school, smarty-pants. This is a fuck-ton harder."

I draw a deep breath, letting it fill me, letting it fuel me. "So I just shut it down?"

He sighs heavily. "I can't tell you to do that. All I can say is be prepared for a hurricane-size storm if you open it up."

I sink back on the bench, certain that Max's advice is spot on. Because it aligns with the woman's wishes—Josie made it perfectly clear from the start that we are temporary, and she laid down the law again last night. "What do I do next? How do I just return to being roommates and friends?"

He drapes an arm around me. "You don't."

I shoot him a look as if he's speaking Swahili. "What?"

"You don't go back. Come stay with me. Take a break before being so close to her drives you crazy. You can move in with her again if you want, but stay with me for a few days, a few weeks, a few months—as long as you want. Whatever you need while you get this shit sorted out."

At first, I want to blow him off. To say "nah, I hardly need that." But something about his idea gives me a sense of calm I haven't felt in a while. The longer I stay with Josie, the harder it'll be when it ends. And it will end. The clock is winding down.

"Maybe I should," I say.

He nods. "I don't pretend to have any answers, but I love you, man. I don't want to see you hurt, and right now, I can tell you are."

I am, and I can't stand feeling this way. I go for my best attempt at humor production. "So, you love me?"

He drops his knuckles to my head and grinds them against my skull. "I do."

"Like a brother?"

He laughs. "Just like a brother."

Right now, maybe that's what I need most.

CHAPTER THIRTY
From the pages of Josie's Recipe Book

Everything But Raisins Cookies

Ingredients

1 1/2 cups all-purpose flour

1 1/4 teaspoons baking soda

1 teaspoon salt

1 1/2 teaspoons ground cinnamon

1 cup butter, softened

1 1/2 cups packed brown sugar

1 cup white sugar

2 eggs

1 1/2 teaspoons vanilla extract

1 cup dried cherries

2 cups rolled oats

1/2 cup flaked coconut

2 cups semisweet chocolate chips

1 cup chopped pecans

Directions

1. Preheat oven to 350 degrees. Grease cookie sheet. Sift together flour, baking soda, salt, and cinnamon.

2. In a large bowl, mix together butter, brown sugar, and white sugar until smooth. Add in the eggs one at a time, beating gently, because if you don't you'll ruin the eggs, and destroy the recipe, and you'll be left with a gigantic bowl of everything cookie dough disappointment that you can't bake and you can't eat either.

3. Stir in vanilla. Mix in the sifted ingredients until well blended. Carefully. Do it carefully. If you screw this up and stir too long, I swear you'll kill it. Do as I say.

4. Using a wooden spoon, mix in the cherries, oats, coconut, chocolate chips, and pecans. This won't be easy, so put a little muscle into it. It's hard, what you're doing. But it'll be even harder if you don't do this properly.

5. Drop cookie batter onto sheets, placing them two inches apart. Now, don't go crazy and get them too close. If you do, you'll have to ditch the whole batch. You don't want that, do you?

6. Bake for eight to ten minutes in preheated oven.

7. While you wait, wipe that stupid tear from your cheek. It's better this way. You know that.

CHAPTER THIRTY-ONE

I have a mind vise, and I'm not afraid to use it.

Even though I've been bitten by the love bug, I can still depend on my special skill—separating emotions from actions as if they're whites and darks in the laundry.

Back at the apartment, I zone in on Josie's hair and only on her hair.

Admittedly, the sharp, chemical odor of hair dye helps matters. Hell, maybe I've found the one thing about her that doesn't turn me on. This shit stinks.

Josie is parked on the closed toilet seat in the bathroom, decked out in leggings and a bra, with a towel draped over her shoulders. I stand behind her, painting pink onto the ends of her hair.

"Do you think this is your new calling?" she asks as I wrap a section of her newly pinked hair in tinfoil. "You seem to be a good hairdresser."

I stop, bend my face near hers, and speak sharply. "If I were you, Miss Josie, I wouldn't be mocking the guy holding a paintbrush full of hair dye."

"I was just teasing," she says softly, but with worry in her tone. "You know that, right?"

"Yes. I do. I'm just giving you a hard time," I tell her, since that's what I have to do to make it through this. Joke, tease, play. Bring us back to who we were before.

"I appreciate you doing this," she says, tilting her face up at me.

Fuck. Those green eyes. Those pretty lips. She makes it too difficult to give her a hard time when all I want to do is kiss her.

But duty calls, and I paint another strand. "I'm not doing this because I have hairdresser aspirations. I'm doing this for you."

She moves her arms behind her and wraps them around my thighs. "Thank you."

Even though all my instincts tell me to drop a kiss on her lips, or whisper something sweet in her ear, I don't listen to them. I ignore them completely and finish her hair.

At some point she lowers her hands and folds them in her lap. Briefly, I wonder if she can feel the tension in the room. If she can sense the shift.

When I'm done, she stands and looks at me. Her eyes are etched with worry—maybe fear, too. "I have to let it sit for twenty minutes. Do you want to watch another episode of *Bored to Death*?"

I say yes, and we settle in next to each other on the couch.

We started bingeing on this HBO show a few days ago. The first time we watched an episode was Tuesday night, after a wildly hot session under the sheets during which we learned that we're one of those couples that not only loves, but is really fucking good at sixty-nine.

Fuck.

I didn't mean *couple.*

But, boy, did we rock that position. Neither one of us skipped a beat. I devoured her sweet pussy while she went to town on my cock, and we climaxed within about sixty seconds of each other.

And now I'm aroused while watching Ted Danson. Great. Fucking great. I'm not even touching Josie, she smells like a chemical factory, and yet the mere memory of her coming on my face is enough to get a hell of a rise out of me.

Hmmm.

Maybe I need one more time with her.

Yeah, I definitely need a final round. We don't have to sixty-nine for me to be a happy camper. Any position will do.

When the show ends and she clicks off the TV, I offer my services. "Want me to rinse that out?"

"Sure."

Back into the bathroom we go. Josie drops the towel from her shoulders and strips off her leggings. She unhooks the bra, and the white lace falls to the tile floor. I strip off my clothes, too, while she turns on the faucet. As the water heats up, I reach behind her head and undo the tinfoil pieces, balling them up and tossing them in the trash.

Then she tips her head toward the shower.

She doesn't have to say it. But I swear I can hear the words on her lips. *One last time.*

Or maybe it's just an echo in my head.

"Ladies first," I say, and open the shower door for her. She stands under the stream, and I join her in the heat as she lets the water rinse out the color. Pinkish waterfalls slide down her body, over her breasts, down her legs. The dye splashes on the tile floor in a bright fuchsia puddle.

I grab her shampoo, pour some in my hand, and lather up her hair. She sighs happily, like a cat being petted. That's one of the very many things I love about this girl. She welcomes touch. She's amazingly good at giving pleasure, and accepting it, too. Not every woman can bask in the moment and savor someone adoring her body. But Josie can. She opens herself fully to feeling good, to being worshipped as she fucking deserves. And it's maddening how much it turns me on.

I concentrate on the task of washing her hair. Once she's all lathered up, I tip her head back and rinse out the shampoo. When her hair is sleek as a seal's, she raises her head out of the stream.

"There," I say, and she opens her eyes and loops her arms around my neck.

She lifts her chin and says a soft, "Thank you."

"Anytime," I say, trying to keep it light, since I feel anything but.

She runs her finger over my top lip as the hot water beats down. "Did you know I'm on the pill?"

All the air rushes from my lungs. I nod. "I did know that."

That's the thing about sharing a bathroom and a medicine cabinet. We don't have too many secrets.

"Do you want to do it without protection?"

I groan, and somehow my dick thickens more, practically begging me to get down to business this second.

Josie is killing me. Just fucking killing me. Max was right. I've got to get out of here. I can't be near her. I can't resist her.

Right now, I don't intend to.

I shift her to the wall, push her back against it, and slide my hand between her legs. I stroke her pussy and marvel at the feel. It hits me that she's this turned on simply from me washing her hair.

212 · LAUREN BLAKELY

Jesus Christ.

In some alternate universe I'm the luckiest bastard on the face of the earth, to have a woman who's so wildly aroused.

In this one, I'm just the schmuck about to enjoy his final benefit.

But make no mistake, I'm going to enjoy the ever-loving hell out of it.

I hook her leg around my hip, holding her tight, then rub my dick against her sweet, wet center. A sexy moan falls from her gorgeous mouth, and I slide home.

It's extraordinary.

And I never want to wear a condom again because this is motherfucking heaven. Her heat envelopes me. Her walls clench around my hard-on. Her breath catches, the most desperate sound I've ever heard her make.

Then I fuck her.

In my head, I say that word over and over.

This is fucking. This is fucking. This is fucking.

This isn't making love.

This is just the final screw before I go. I can't care about the way she threads her hands in my hair. I can't linger on the murmurs she makes. And I can't give a second thought ever again to how she clutches me and cries my name when she comes, as if I'm the answer to her every wish.

I won't let myself think about how she sounds just as lost as I am.

Because seconds later, I'm coming, too, and the pleasure blots out the empty ache.

* * *

A little later I'm dried off and dressed. I zip up my backpack, which contains a few changes of clothes. Footsteps sound behind me, then a question.

"What are you doing?"

I turn around, take a breath, and rip off the Band-Aid like I promised I'd do. "I'm going to stay with Max."

Her jaw drops. "What?"

I nod. "Just for a little while."

"Why?" Her brow furrows as her voice wobbles. She stands in my doorway, dressed in jeans and a cute green blouse. Her hair is blown dry, and the ends are bright pink now.

I step closer. "I think the cake is baked now, baby," I say softly, remembering I have to do this. "It'll be easier this way."

"You're just leaving?"

"I'll be back. I promise." Though, right now I don't know how to be near her when I want her this badly. "We always knew we had to stop. I can't stop when I'm living in the same six hundred square feet as you. It feels like we're playing house."

She bites her lip as if she's holding in all her sadness. "You think we're just playing house?"

I glance around and wave at the walls, frustration building inside me, mixed with hurt. "We can't just go on like this," I say. Then I can't help it. I'm done. I just can't hold it in anymore. I unleash my heart. "I wake up next to you, and I want to touch you. I watch TV with you, and I can't stop kissing you. Hell, I dye your hair and we wind up naked in the shower. I can't just cut this off like it's a growth and go back to watching *Bored to Death* without wanting to make love to you," I say, then wince because I've made my great mistake.

I swallow nervously, but stand my ground.

Her eyes pin me, and she says nothing for a moment that lasts too long. When she speaks, her tone is soft and tender. "Was that what it was for you?"

I won't go first. "You tell me." My voice is gravelly. Broken.

She crosses her arms. She doesn't answer me. Instead, she purses her lips then speaks softly. "I don't want you to leave."

I reach for her elbow, desperation spiraling in me. But I'm not even sure what I'm fighting for—for her to see what we could become, or for her to let me go. "You want to stay friends, don't you?"

She nods. "You know I do."

I grip her arm tighter. "And you said this had to end. Josie, it's too hard for me to be here right now. You've got to understand."

A tear slides down her cheek. Then one trickles over the other. More fall, like a summer rain shower. She swipes at her cheeks, but she's fighting an uphill battle.

I'm torn between wanting to pull her in my arms and comfort her and needing to protect myself. But there's something else at play, too. Morbid curiosity. That wins. "Josie," I say, and she draws a sharp inhale and looks up. "Was it that way for you?"

She parts her lips, but no answer comes because a loud rap of knuckles reverberates through the apartment.

"Did you order lunch or something?" I ask.

She shakes her head and turns on her heel, heading for the door. "The doorman called a few minutes ago. He had to take care of something on our floor so he offered to bring up the package."

The knocking continues. "Ah, your rolling pin."

"Probably." Her voice is empty.

She peers through the peephole then nods at me. She unlocks and opens the door. A short, stout man in a green blazer stands at the threshold. The day doorman.

"Ms. Hammer, this is for you," he says, then hands her a white envelope. The legal size.

She regards it curiously. "What is this?"

"I signed for it yesterday. It's a certified letter."

He turns to go, and she lets the door fall closed. She looks at me then at the envelope. I shrug and gesture to the item in her hand. *Open it.* She takes out a sheet of paper and reads.

After a minute, she blinks and meets my eyes. "It's from the landlord." Her voice is a barren whisper.

"What did he say?"

"Mr. Barnes needs the apartment for his niece," she says heavily, then shakes her head like she can't believe the hand she was just dealt. "We have to be out in a month. We're losing our home."

Looks like our days of playing house truly are over.

CHAPTER THIRTY-TWO
From the pages of Josie's Recipe Book

Josie's Misery Salad

Ingredients

Lettuce

Tomatoes

Carrots

Whatever

1. Wash lettuce. Even on days like this you don't want to eat unwashed lettuce.

2. Slice some tomatoes like you fucking care.

3. Cut up some carrots. Doesn't even matter if you peel them.

4. Toss some oil and vinegar in it. Or don't. Whatever.

5. Eat it, especially since you need to punish yourself more. You totally effed up. You know you did. Where do we even start? Everywhere. From the beginning right on through to the other day when you watched him walk out the door. Idiot. You don't deserve sweets.

CHAPTER THIRTY-THREE

I'd like to say I bury myself in work that next week, but that would do a disservice to every other day I've tended to a wound, or stitched up a knee, or removed a mustard jar from a butt.

Hey, it's a dirty job but someone's got to do it.

Anyway, work saves me.

I've always buried myself in it, but I like to think that's the only way to do the job. To give all of myself to it. I'm glad I have a job that demands everything of me. Mercy gets not only one hundred percent of my focus, but one hundred and ten percent. Maybe this is the real lucky-bastard life—to have a job I love so much that I don't even have time to think about the girl I miss. At the end of each work day, I'm relieved I've logged ten or twelve hours without thinking about her.

The trouble is my shift ends every evening.

That's when the missing begins in earnest, pain like a phantom limb, a persistent reminder of what I don't have anymore.

One night after work, Wyatt texts me to meet up with him and Nick, telling me it's softball season and I need to get my ass to Central Park.

I go, and I'm both grateful and really fucking depressed that Josie's not playing this year. Nick hits a home run; that's par for the course for him. I manage a small degree of satisfaction when I knock in two runners during my turn at bat.

That feeling fades, though, when I leave, head downtown, and check my phone. There's no note from Josie. I sigh heavily as I flop down on the couch at Max's home, absently fiddling with the screen. I could write to her. I could text her. I *should*.

But it's too fucking hard. I didn't even see her when I stopped by the apartment a few days ago to grab the rest of my things. I made sure to go when I knew she'd be at work.

When Max comes home with Chinese takeout and beer, I switch off the Josie portion of my brain and turn on the hunger lobe. That does the trick, and I do find a small degree of pleasure in knowing I'm returning to old habits. I haven't completely lost my dependable talent for compartmentalization. It's like a renaissance of sorts, as I'm remade back into the guy who isn't head over heels for a girl.

Yup. I know this dude. I can be this dude. As I put my feet on Max's coffee table, I stretch my arms, my old self coming back.

He kicks off my foot. "Dude, this isn't a frat house."

"Josie let me do it," I grumble.

He arches an eyebrow. "Josie doesn't make the rules here." He grabs the clicker and flicks on the TV, scrolling to HBO. "You seen the newest *Ballers* episode? This show kills it."

I groan and slide my hand over my face.

"What? You don't like the Rock?"

"No, that's not it."

"Don't tell me it reminds you of Josie."

Busted.

"Maybe," I mutter.

"You should text her. See her. You're supposed to be friends with her. Be fucking friends with her."

"She hasn't texted me, though, except about keys and the apartment."

He smacks the back of my head. "What are you? Twelve?" He grabs my phone from the table and shoves it at me. "Call her. Have a coffee or whatever you do with her that doesn't involve keys or the apartment or household shit." He sets his laser-beam eyes to high. "Or I'll do it for you."

That does the trick. I send her a note, asking her if she wants to have breakfast tomorrow. She says she'll be leaving early for work, but suggests dinner or drinks in the evening.

We settle on drinks. And it's weird—Josie and I were never the friends who went out to get drinks. We sampled food. We saw movies. We wandered in and out of bookstores. We walked and talked and tried her bakery goods.

I don't want to get a brew with her.

But I do it anyway, meeting her the next day at Speakeasy in Midtown. She's already at the bar when I walk in. Perched on a stool, her legs are crossed, and she wears pink sandals, a purple skirt with a candy pattern on it, and a white tank top.

My skin heats up, and I have to reel in all my dirty thoughts. Mainly the ones that remind me exactly what she looks like underneath those clothes. How she feels. How she tastes. How she moves, and moans, and groans, and for fuck's sake, brain, have a little mercy on a man. Some things are not fair, like planting those alluring images in my head right now.

I walk over to her, and it's awkward for a moment. Then she hops off the stool and throws her arms around me. "Hey you."

"Hey you," I echo and pump a virtual fist. We can do this.

She holds up a hand like a stop sign. "Before we order, I have this for you." She reaches into her bag and grabs a treat.

Old times. Yes. We are back to the way we were. "Can't wait."

"It's a mini cinnamon bun. It's like a cinnamon bun met a cookie."

"And they had babies."

She laughs. "They totally did. They got it on in the oven and made delicious cinnamony, sugary children. Try it."

"Bringing food into a bar. You scofflaw."

She brings her finger to her lips. "Shhh."

She hands the small treat to me, and it's one of the sweetest things I've ever tasted. "Your mini bun is amazing," I say, and I'm rewarded with her smile. "And yes, I do know that sounded dirty."

"It did, and I'm glad you said it, and glad you like it." She leans closer, a playful look in her eyes. "Confession: I've always had a thing for cinnamon."

This is news to me, and I'm digging that she's sharing pieces of herself, just the same as before. "That so? Tell me more."

She shrugs lightly. "It makes me feel as if I can do anything."

"So it's like a good drug?"

"Exactly." She pats my knee like she used to do. "I'm glad we're doing this."

"Yeah, me, too." Because some Josie is better than no Josie. "Hey, have you ever made a peanut butter brownie?"

"Like with peanut butter in a chocolate brownie?"

I tap my nose. "Yes."

"I have, but not recently."

"Put that on your afternoon special. That would be amazing."

She mimes writing a note, and the bartender swings by to take our orders. When he leaves, we chat, like two old friends catching up. "How's everything? How's the place?"

"Actually," she begins, taking her time. "I already moved out. After you picked up your things."

"Whoa. That was fast. You don't let the body get cold."

"It just made sense."

"Did you get a new place already? I'm jealous that your real estate mojo is that good."

She shakes her head. "I moved some of the furniture to my parents' storage unit. Well, Wyatt moved it, since he has a truck," she says, and I feel like an ass that her brother helped her rather than me.

"Sorry I wasn't there to lend a hand."

A small smile appears on her face. "It's no big deal. It was easy enough. And now I'm staying with Lily till I figure things out. Since she kicked out Rob, she's got room for me."

Lily and Josie. Two lovely single ladies living together. My radar goes off. "Are you dating again?"

She gives me a look that can only be read as *you ass*. "Seriously?"

I swallow, trying to play it cool. "Aren't we allowed to talk about that? We did before."

She nods.

"So, that's a yes? You're dating?" Jealousy flares in me like wildfire, a hot, raging beast.

She narrows her eyes. "I was acknowledging we used to talk about dating," she says, clearly affronted by my questions. "What about you? Are you dating?"

I huff, then scoff for good measure. "No. Hell no."

"Then why would I be?" she asks, holding her hands out wide in a question.

"You wanted to before," I point out.

"Things changed." She bites out each word.

Yeah, "things" as in everything.

She takes a deep breath as if she's calming herself down. "Okay, let's start over." She smiles cheerily at me. "How's work?"

We talk about work, and only work, like everything else is off the table. Maybe it should be. When it's time to leave, we walk out together and stand awkwardly on the sidewalk, rocking on our heels.

"Chase?"

My heart beats faster from the way she says my name. "Yeah?" I ask like that one word contains all the hope in my universe.

She smiles wistfully. "I miss you."

The hope dissipates. I wanted more than missing. But I answer her truthfully. "I miss you, too."

"We should do this again," she says.

"Absolutely."

Because we're friends and this is what we wanted. This is what we planned for.

She drops a quick kiss to my cheek before she walks away.

I'm not sure if I like our new normal any more than I liked being without her.

CHAPTER THIRTY-FOUR

On Thursday night, Max and I head to the newest Lucky Spot. Business has been booming for Spencer and Charlotte, and they just expanded their bar in the heart of Chelsea, adding on a Ping-Pong table room. On Monday and Wednesday nights, the bar hosts leagues for the sport, and Thursday is a themed night featuring Ping-Pong and champagne.

Wyatt and Natalie called everyone together for a post-wedding evening out. I'm not sure if it's their third or fourth wedding to each other, or just another excuse for them to celebrate being married. The two of them like doing that, and so the gang's all here.

That also means this is the first time Josie and I have hung out with the whole group of friends since the end of our short-lived stretch as roommates and an even briefer stint as lovers. But no one else knows about the latter except Max.

As we walk along Eighteenth Street, I remind him. "Keep it on the down-low in front of everyone, okay?"

He stage-whispers, "You mean about you having a big thing for Josie Hammer?"

"Yes," I say through gritted teeth.

"Got it. Because no one else could ever fucking tell." He yanks open the door to the bar, and we stroll inside, joining the crew in the Ping-Pong room.

Instantly, my eyes find her. Josie rests her hip against the green Ping-Pong table. She wears a red skirt, and little ankle boots that would look fantastic parked on my shoulders. Wrapped around my neck. Hooked around my waist.

I drag a hand through my hair and fix on a friendly smile, lest anyone catch on that I was cycling through my favorite positions.

Josie holds a glass of champagne as she chats with Natalie. The two of them watch Harper as she bounces on her toes at one end of the table, a paddle in her hand. From the other end, Nick serves the white plastic ball, and the two volley for the next minute. Nick is ferociously focused, slamming the ball back at her each time, but then Harper delivers a punishing blow to the right corner, and when Nick stretches to reach it, the ball rattles to the floor.

Harper thrusts her arms in the air. "The streak continues!"

Josie holds her flute high, toasting Harper's victory. Natalie hoots and hollers.

A new couple strolls through the doorway and into the Ping-Pong room—she's a petite blonde with wavy, honey-colored hair, and the guy towers over her, a tall and broad dude. The woman chimes in, "Nick, you can never beat her. Don't you know that by now?"

Nick pushes his glasses up his nose and shrugs. "But I can't stop trying, Abby."

"Better luck next time," the new guy says with a smile.

Harper steps in and introduces me to her friends Simon and Abby. After we all shake hands, Simon drapes an arm around Abby's shoulders and plants a kiss on her cheek, for no obvious reason other than he can. Lucky fucker.

As I peer around, I see nothing but couples. Natalie and Wyatt, Spencer and Charlotte, Nick and Harper, Simon and Abby. It's just the Summers brothers who are single, and Josie. The thing is, Max is happy with his status, as far as I can tell. In principle, I don't object to mine. I was never bothered being a one-man operation. Until I fell for Josie.

Now, seeing all these paired-up friends reminds me that I'm the one of us who didn't get the woman he wanted.

Wyatt drops a hand to my shoulder. "Ready to be decimated?" he asks as he hands me a paddle.

"I am ready," I say confidently, taking a deliberate beat, "to obliterate you."

He arches a brow, like I can't possibly be serious. But I am, because bar games and me are a winning combination. Tonight, the game has a welcome side effect. Beating Wyatt's sorry ass keeps me from staring at his sister all night.

"Bastard," he mutters as I slam the winning ball in our second round, since he challenged me to a rematch after I pummeled him in the first. Foolish choice on his part.

But before I can trash-talk Wyatt about his second loss, Spencer's voice booms across the room. "What are you two cats doing about living arrangements now that the landlord gave you the screw?"

The man is aces at bringing up the elephant in the room, even unintentionally. Spencer looks at me, then Josie.

She pipes up first. "I'm living with a friend."

"Lots of pillow fights and late-night gab fests?" he asks. "Or do you style each other's hair? Color it even? Bake cookies and watch HBO?"

Josie meets my gaze from the other side of the Ping-Pong table. A tiny smile lifts her lips, a private one that I know is just for me. I answer her with a small quirk of my lips, too. There's a mischievous sparkle in her eyes.

But then the hint of secrets shared is extinguished and replaced by something else entirely. Resolve? Acceptance? I can't tell anymore.

She nods as she meets Spencer's waiting stare. "Yes, that's exactly what we do. All night sessions."

I don't know if the innuendo is for me, or just to needle Spencer. That's the problem. She feels so close, but so far out of reach.

Spencer turns to me and raises his chin. "And what about you? How's life at Chez Summers Brothers? Keeping busy watching monster truck rallies and avoiding all food that requires utensils?"

I look around for Max, but he's disappeared. "Yeah, it's one big fiesta of masculine stereotypes. Some nights we beat our chests like Tarzan."

Charlotte laughs. "I bet you miss the feminine touch Josie brought to living together."

Boy, do I ever. Charlotte's words are like a punch in the chest.

Once more our eyes lock, and I try to find the answer in Josie's light green gaze. But I don't even know what I'm looking for. "Yeah," I say, since I can't manage a joke right now.

Wyatt raises a beer. "But it was good while it lasted, though, right?"

He doesn't even know the half of it. I swallow and answer him. "It was the best."

Josie nibbles on the corner of her lip and looks away. Harper jumps in, and her voice seems protective, as if she's watching out for Josie. "I'm sure it was." She hoists her paddle high above her head. "Anyone up for another round? Or are you all too chicken to take on the Ping-Pong champion?"

That riles up Spencer, who grabs a paddle from Nick. As they play, Max wanders back in, his jaw set, his eyes blazing.

"Everything good?" I ask him.

He shakes his head and mutters, "Had to take a phone call." He scrubs a hand across his jaw. "Fucking Henley Rose."

I raise an eyebrow. I haven't heard that name in ages. "Your former apprentice?"

With a heavy sigh, he shoots me a can-you-believe-it look. "That's the one."

Color me surprised. "The one who left you for your competitor in a fit of you'll-rue-the-day-you-let-me-go anger?"

"Thanks for the reminder of her parting words."

"Would it be easier if I reminded you that you thought she was smoking hot, and your greatest accomplishment each day was not staring at her every single second she was under the engine or bent over the hood?"

He narrows his eyes. "Nothing ever happened with her," he says through gritted teeth.

"So what was the call about then?"

He gives me a ten-second overview of the call, and my jaw drops. "Well, that's going to make for one hell of a tawdry tale."

He claps my back. "But that's a story for another time."

"I look forward to that time then," I say, since I can't wait to hear more about the woman who drove my brother crazy once upon a time.

A few minutes later, after Harper bests her cocky brother, she circles by, pointing to a low table in the corner of the room next to some comfy emerald green chairs. "They've got Scrabble back here. Want to play?"

Max shakes his head. "Nah."

But Scrabble is hard for me to resist, and I'm sure Harper knows my weakness. She nudges me. "What about you, Chase? You and Josie are a good combo, right?"

From a few feet away, Josie chimes in, "We're the best. We beat the Hammer twins every time."

Harper rubs her hands together. "I can't wait to see that." She tips her chin to the game by the chairs. "Show us how good you can be."

Nick grabs a chair and flips open the board. "Or don't you think you can beat us, Doctor Brain?"

I have no choice. I must destroy him now. "Those are fighting words, Nick. Prepare to die on the Scrabble board. A slow, painful death wrought by triple word scores and more combinations with *J* and *X* than you can even begin to spell."

Josie cracks up. "Yes, dear brothers. We play to kill."

And we do.

We win with a final combination of "onerous" and the "ex" that Josie builds on our final turn.

I try to read nothing into it. It's just a two-letter word.

When everyone else is busy doing couple stuff, she rests a hand on my arm. "I'm glad we can do this, Chase. I'm glad we're still friends. Are you?"

"Absolutely. I'm stoked we're friends, too."

But she's also something else. She's an ex, and that's a whole other thing. I'm learning being friends with an ex isn't the same as being friends with a woman.

Once you've crossed the line into lovers, everything changes. Returning to the way you were before isn't easy.

It's onerous.

CHAPTER THIRTY-FIVE

From the pages of Josie's Recipe Book

Josie's Liquid Courage

Ingredients

Coffee

Cinnamon

Courage

1. Brew your best Ethiopian coffee in a coffeemaker.

2. Pour into your favorite mug. Stir in cinnamon. Add a dollop of cream.

3. Get ready. You can do anything.

CHAPTER THIRTY-SIX

That Sunday, Max and I finish the century. Our team comes in third, and we raise a few thousand dollars for veterans. Not too shabby for two dudes who aren't pro cyclists.

The next morning he leaves for a car show, and on the way to work I finish an audiobook on the role of randomness in our lives (spoiler: chance is everything). At the hospital, I start my shift with a patient who's suffering from an early case of the flu. We treat her and then move on to a boy with a broken arm. They're textbook cases, and we take care of them.

Everything feels as normal as it can possibly be. Amazing, how you can think you won't survive a broken heart, but experience has taught me that you always do. You just keep moving forward. Life goes on, and during my lunch break with David, I grab a turkey sandwich from the cafeteria and get in line to pay. Out of the corner of my eye, I spot an orthopedic surgeon I know as he unfolds a brown lunch bag and takes out a tuna fish sandwich. My first instinct is to text Josie that I've spotted someone in the wild eating our least favorite food.

Briefly, I wonder if I can still do that. If I *should* do that. And the fact that I don't know the right answer gnaws at my gut.

But then it's my turn to pay. As I open my wallet to grab some bills, a business card falls out. I grab it from the counter next to the cashier and flip it over. Kevin's card. Right. He included it when he gave me the cooking class certificate.

Oh shit.

I never thanked him for the class.

When I finish my turkey sandwich, I push away from the table, and tell David I need to go. Out in the corridor, I lob in a call, and Kevin's receptionist puts me through right away when I say who I am.

"Dr. Summers, how the hell are you? I hope you aren't calling to tell me you found something suspicious in an old forehead X-ray of mine?"

I laugh and shake my head. "Nope, and call me Chase. Anyway, I wanted to say thank you for the class. That was nice of you to do. We had a great time."

"Awesome. Did you get engaged, too?"

I stop in my tracks in front of the MRI room. "What? No. Why? I just went with a friend."

"Ah, that's cool. I was just messing with you, since Cassidy and I got engaged that night."

"Because of the class?" I ask, resuming my pace toward the stairwell.

"Yes, and we owe you. That's one of the reasons we wanted to thank you when we came by a few weeks ago. Your suggestion to take that cooking class was exactly what I needed. Something just clicked for me that night at Enticing Appetizers. I knew Cassidy was the one for me forever. And the next night I proposed."

As an orderly pushes a med cart down the corridor, I back against the wall, giving him room. "Huh," I say, taking in Kevin's news. "So it all became clear?"

"Like crystal."

I flash back to the night Josie and I attended the quirky class, and how we made our great escape, fleeing from Ivory and then rumbling uptown on the subway, heading home. How, there on the train, Josie rested her head on my shoulder and threaded her hand in mine.

And it was clear.

Then later at our house, she took care of me when I twisted my ankle.

And it was clear.

A part of me knew then. A part of me was damn sure that she felt the same wild and crazy way I did. And I didn't say enough at the time to hold on to her. I didn't go out on a limb.

I took the safe option, not the risky, daring, hallelujah one.

Something else is clear right now, too. I haven't moved on. I'm not over her. And I definitely don't want to be just friends with Josie.

I want to know I can text her about a goddamn tuna fish sandwich, and I want to send that message as her man. I don't want to fire it off as her favorite guy friend. I want to tell her about the tuna, then take her out to dinner and wander around the city with her, hand in hand. After that I want to go home with her, fall into bed with her, and love her.

That's what I wanted a few weeks ago when I moved out. My heart, for her, hasn't changed.

But what's crystal clear now is that the bigger risk isn't losing her as a friend. The bigger risk is losing the woman I'm pretty damn sure is the love of my life.

"Hey Kevin, can you help me with something?" I ask, remembering the corporate name on his business card. The guy's job might be just the ticket. He's got to know people, right?

"Anything. Name it."

I tell him what I need, and he says, "Consider it done."

When we hang up, I send Josie a text.

Chase: Hey! Any chance I can stop by the bakery when my shift ends? I have something for you.

Her response comes a minute later.

Josie: Yes. I have something for you, too.

* * *

There's someone else I need to talk to first. I text Wyatt and he gives me the address where he's working today.

The second my shift ends, I hop on my bike in my scrubs and ride across town to Wyatt's job site, adrenaline fueling me, turning me back into the speed demon I've always been. He's remodeling a kitchen in a brownstone in the West Eighties, and he comes to the door and lets me into the foyer.

"What's the deal? You said it was mission critical," he says, a hammer in his hand, his tool belt on.

My breath comes fast and hard from the two-wheeled sprint. "Yes. It's critical." I cut to the chase. "I need you to know I'm in love with your sister."

He scoffs and runs his free hand over his chin. "Tell me something I don't know."

My jaw drops. "What? How did you know?"

He clasps my shoulder and laughs. "Dude, everyone knows that. The question now is: Are you finally going to do something about it?"

I can barely contain a grin. "Yes. I'm going to do something about it. Are you okay with it? If you're not, I'm sorry, but not sorry. I'm going to tell her anyway. Even so, I wanted you to know before I do it."

He laughs. "Appreciate the heads-up. And when I asked you to look out for her, it was to protect her from jackasses. I'm pretty sure you're not one of them. I'm also pretty sure this isn't the kind of story where the fact that you're in love with your buddy's sister holds you back. The hurdle has always been how much the two of you already care about each other," he says, and squeezes my shoulder harder. "Besides, I approve of you so much it's ridiculous. Now, stop talking to me, and go see my sister. See if you can become her favorite person in the universe."

That's exactly what I want to be for her.

"Thanks, man," I say, then we hug. But, you know, a manly hug.

I leave. But when I reach Sunshine Bakery, take off my helmet and lock up my bike by a meter, I pat the pockets of my scrubs and curse. What the hell is wrong with me? I'm showing up empty-handed. That's not how you win a woman's heart.

I spin around, looking for something. *Anything.*

When my eyes land on a sea of white and yellow, I'm struck with the memory of giving her daisies. That seems far too long ago. But this time, the gift has another purpose. I buy a bouquet from her friend's flower shop, and as I reach the door of the bakery, my heart jackhammers.

Excitement trips through me, and a full dose of nervousness races alongside it, too. I don't know how she feels, what she'll say, or what she'll do.

But I know the possibility of an *us* is worth the risk.

This once felt like a hallelujah scenario.

Now it is the only option.

CHAPTER THIRTY-SEVEN

The closed sign rests on the door, but I knock twice. Looking up from her post behind the counter, Josie smiles, wipes her hands on her apron, and heads to the door. Unlocking it, she lets me in. Her hair is swept back in a ponytail, and her lips shine with gloss.

I waste no time.

"Yes," I say emphatically. Loudly. Confidently.

"Yes what?"

"Every time we were together, it felt like making love. Every time. All the time. Every night," I say, and her green eyes twinkle instantly, as if they've been lit up by my words. "That's because I fell in love with you before we even slept together."

"You did?" she asks, her voice feather-soft and full of wonder. I recognize the sound because it's how I feel when I look at her.

"I'm crazy about you. I want Swedish Fish with you all the time. I don't want to be on the other side of the wall in an apartment with you." I wave toward downtown, where Max lives. "And I definitely don't want to be all the way on the other side of the city. Right now, it feels like a million miles separate us, and I can't stand it."

"I can't stand it, either," she says, her voice shaking, and she steps closer. I set the flowers on the nearest table and take her hands in mine.

I meet her gaze. Her green eyes are the only ones I want to get lost in. "I want to be the one you come home to and wake up to. I want to buy toilet paper for you, and go to Bed Bath & Beyond to shop for sheets for a bed that we share." Her lips quiver, and her shoulders tremble as I go on. "I want to come home to find you in an apron that makes you even more impossible to resist, and I don't want to ever resist you again."

She nods over and over, tears slipping down her cheeks. And everything is right in the world again. Everything is miraculous. Everything is good once more because what I thought she was feeling in the cooking class is true. It's clear. It's real.

"Don't resist me." She grabs the neck of my shirt. "I love you so much."

And my heart, it doesn't just pump blood through the body now. It's a rocket, and it soars straight through the atmosphere and keeps going. It's no longer an organ that simply sustains all the vital functions in the body. It's the one that plays the most vital role of all—loving her.

I dip my mouth to hers, tasting her sweetness, savoring the closeness. Her kiss is cupcake and frosting, sex and love. It's everything that turns me on, and everything I need to be happy.

Her.

I've missed it, and I can't get enough. I kiss her deeper, threading my hand in her hair, then at last letting go.

When we break the kiss, I feel as if I'm floating. As if this is my new normal. And I'm so damn glad I told her, because the chance to be with the one you want—the one who wants you the same damn way—is worth the risk.

I run the backs of my fingers along her soft cheek. "The thing is, I think I've been in love with you for a long time, Josie. I think I was falling for you since before I left the country. Now that I'm back, both my brother and your brother laughed at me when I told them I loved you, like it was the most obvious thing in the world."

Her smile is as wide as the sky. "I've been crazy about you for a long time, too, and I think it took living together for my heart to hit my brain over the head and make me realize it fully."

"Yeah?" I smile dopily. I don't ever want to come down from this high.

She ropes her arms around my neck, her fingers playing with the ends of my hair, like she did that night on the train. "Last night I was looking back through my recipes—ones I've written out in the last few months. I wrote a bunch about you, and it was kind of obvious when I read them that I've had a big thing for you for a while."

I grind against her for a second. "I've got a big thing for you," I say, and she laughs. Then I add more seriously, "I'd love to see those someday. Your recipes."

"I'd love to show them to you. This morning, I wrote a coffee recipe with cinnamon."

A new sort of happiness floods my chest because I know why this girl likes cinnamon. I love being privy to all the quirks of Josie. From tuna to cinnamon, from sharing her heart to sharing her home, from sixty-nine to self-love. "Because cinnamon makes you feel like you can do anything?"

She nods. "And today, I wanted the courage to tell you how I felt. Then you showed up and said the same."

I laugh lightly. "Were we just stupid for not saying a thing before?"

She shakes her head. "No. I think we both loved each other too much as friends to risk losing the other person. But then, I think being apart from you was its own kind of loss. That's why I told you I had something for you. Something new I made."

She hands me a bakery bag, the kind she's always given me, and I'm floored once more by this woman. Josie's always giving me gifts, and I can't lie—it makes me outrageously happy to be the recipient.

I read the note first. "Josie's All-In Chocolate Peanut Butter Brownies," I say with a smile.

"Credit given where credit is due. They were your idea."

Then I read the recipe that's printed on the note.

Ingredients

2 cups chocolate chips

1 cup butter

1/2 cup peanut butter

1/2 teaspoon vanilla extract

1 1/4 cups all-purpose flour

1 cup white sugar

3 eggs, beaten

2 teaspoons baking soda

1/4 teaspoon salt

Directions

1. Preheat oven to 350 degrees and grease a baking dish as you prepare to lay your heart on the line.

2. Melt the chocolate chips, butter, and peanut butter together, like how everything melted when you fell in love with Chase. Stir frequently to avoid burning. Yes, you were worried about this before, but now there's something bigger at stake.

3. Stir vanilla, flour, sugar, eggs, baking soda, and salt into the chocolate mixture. Pour batter into baking dish. This is the brand-new blend, and nothing is separated anymore. Time to accept that love and friendship and sex and happiness have all come together.

4. Bake brownies in the preheated oven until ready. Cool to room temperature before cutting into squares. Serve to the one guy you want—the one you hope wants you the same way.

I look up from the paper and at my girl.

She's mine.

"Does this mean I can have the brownie now and eat it, too?"

A naughty glint flickers in her eyes, and lust clambers through me. I half want to kick myself for not telling her I loved her sooner, but I know we came to this on our terms, in the right time, once the friendship alone was no longer enough.

I reach inside the bag, break off a corner of the treat, and eat it. I moan in culinary delight. "This is the second-best thing I've ever tasted."

"What's first?"

I curl my hand around her head. "You."

Then I kiss her, and she's everything I missed, everything I want, and everything I love.

She kisses me back with a tenderness and a fierceness that I now know comes from her whole heart. Josie's always given all of herself, even when she tried to hold back. I once thought I could keep everything in separate drawers, but maybe I'm not that different from her after all.

This blend the two of us have going on is pretty damn good. I like life better when we're together.

Right now there's something I'd like even more, and that's all of her.

I break the kiss and glance around the shop. "How many health codes would we break if we got it on at this place?"

She smiles. "Come to my office."

I wiggle my eyebrows as she locks the front door. "I like the sound of that."

Taking my hand, she guides me to a cubicle in the back. She perches on the edge of a desk that's covered in papers and envelopes, presumably invoices and bills. She pulls me close, and I slam my mouth to hers, kissing her hard and rough, the kind of kiss that leads to only one thing.

Soon, I lift her skirt, tug down her panties, and slide inside.

Her name is a dirty growl on my lips. "Josie. I fucking love you."

She draws me impossibly closer and whispers in my ear, "I fucking love you, too. And, yes, it was always that way for me, too."

We're fast, and we're frenzied, and soon we're both over the edge.

After, I help her close the bakery for the night and we head for the door. "Wait." I stop at the table. "I have a gift for you, too."

I hand her the flowers. "You might be thinking, 'He's not very creative, since he gave me these before.' But last time I gave you flowers, you said they'd make our place cheery. This time I got them for you because I want to live with you again. In a new place. Just for us. One you can make cheery with these flowers." Her eyes seem to sparkle as she waits for me to say more. "Would you like to live with me again? As my girlfriend?"

She takes my hand. "I would love to."

EPILOGUE

Five months later

The apartment hunt didn't last long this time.

Nothing was cursed. No one was crazy. I didn't have to sell a spleen or a kidney, either.

As it turns out, all I had to do was remove a piece of a chandelier from a guy's forehead and then stitch it up without a trace.

Kevin hooked me up. Who knew that one day Aquaman would stumble into my ER with a three-inch shard of glass in his forehead, and a beautiful bond would form. I'd fix his face and send him on the path to safer sexcapades. He would wind up engaged and return the favor by connecting me with some of his real estate contacts. One of his real estate guys found a one-bedroom for us in Chelsea that costs an arm and a leg. But somehow we're making it all work, doing our best every day.

Josie's bakery is thriving. Her afternoon specials have lured in many new customers, and they're loving her mini cinnamon buns, the chocolate peanut butter brownies, the candy sushi, and even the grapefruit macarons. Nothing with raisins, though. Thank the Lord.

But tonight, she's not cooking.

I am.

Not gonna lie. Cooking has never been my forte. But learning has. I tracked down some recipes, watched a few videos, practiced a couple of times, and now I'm making her dinner.

I whip up the pasta primavera I've planned for the menu. It's a simple dish, but it's her favorite, and seeing as she treats me like a king in the kitchen, I want to treat her like a queen.

When she walks in the door to our home, she lifts her nose high and inhales. "Mmm," she says in a sexy purr. "Smells good. Somebody's getting lucky tonight."

I leave the kitchen, wrap an arm around her waist, and kiss her. "Had I only known cooking dinner was the way to get in your pants, I'd have done it sooner."

She laughs and drops another kiss on my lips. "Can you imagine? You'd be getting it three times a day instead of once or twice."

Yeah, we're regulars.

Every night. Sometimes every morning, too, even though we rarely get out of bed at the same time. But that doesn't hinder the pursuit of orgasms, since synchronized wake-up calls aren't necessary for sleepy morning sex, and that's a habit we both enjoy.

After she sets down her purse and washes her hands, we eat the dinner I made. When we're done, I clear my throat. "Josie, there's something I want to tell you."

Her eyes widen. "Yes?"

I clasp my hand over hers, then frown. "It's about dessert. I have bad news."

She goes along with my trumped-up concern. "You baked a cake and it fell? You used too much salt in the brownies? Wait. No. Don't tell me you made something with raisins."

I shudder. "Never. But I want to be truthful with you." I inhale deeply, piling it on. "The crème brûlée on the menu? I didn't make it with a crème brûlée torch. In fact, crème brûlée is really fucking hard to make. Confession—I bought it."

She cracks up and runs her hand through my hair. "I forgive you, and I won't even throat-punch you."

I gesture to the kitchen. "Any chance I can trouble you to grab it, though? I just need to gather up the plates."

"Of course." She rises and heads to the kitchen, and with lightning speed, I race to the couch, grab a board from underneath it, and carry it ever-so-carefully with my steady hands to the table.

When I set it down, every tile I laid out earlier is still in place.

And when Josie emerges from the kitchen, I'm in place, too—down on one knee, with a jewelry box in my hand.

She gasps and points to the table, her mouth falling open. She gawks at the Scrabble board. The words on it don't connect with each other like in a crossword puzzle. But they don't have to. I'm not trying to win a double-word score. I want to win her heart forever, and that's why four words, and four words only, are spelled out. I say them out loud. "Will you marry me?"

I flip open the box and present a sparkling diamond ring. "I love you madly, Josie Hammer. Will you be more than my roommate, more than my girlfriend? You're already my best friend. Will you be my wife?"

"Yes," she says, and throws her arms around me, kissing me as tears fall down her cheeks. "I can't wait for you to be my husband."

"Me, too," I say, taking out the diamond.

She holds out her hand, and I slide the ring on her finger. "I guess I'm the one getting lucky tonight," she says with a joyful grin on her face.

The same is true for me, especially since every night, after we engage in our favorite hobby, she lets my hand be Lyle Lyle.

Soon, that hand will have a ring on it.

ANOTHER EPILOGUE

A little later

Let's say, for the sake of argument, that you've fallen madly in love with your best friend. You'd thank your lucky stars you took the chance on living together, right?

If we hadn't been stuck between the rock and the hard place of New York City real estate, I'm not sure we would have combusted the way we did. Living in a mere six hundred square feet with Josie made it impossible to miss what was right in front of me—the woman of my dreams.

I used to think I was the king of compartmentalizing. I thought I could handle romance the way I have to treat my emotions about a patient. But moving in with my best friend taught me that some things are better when they're not separate.

Like desires and actions.

Lust and feelings.

Love and sex.

One used to go *here*. The other went *there*. But everything collided head-on with Josie, smashing together in a potent blend. Looking back, am I ever glad she needed a boob friend the night she slipped into my bed. That one night led to this great love, and now she's my wife.

Sometimes she calls me the full package, the thing she said she was looking for. "I love your brain, and your heart, and your smile, and I especially love *this* part," she'll say, then she'll get a little frisky. Which is fine by me. "But most of all, I love that you're my terrible-singing, innuendo-delivering, sweets-loving, big-hearted Doctor McHottie husband who takes care of me in every way."

And you know, I've got it pretty bad for my bold and daring, bright and beautiful, heart-on-her-sleeve, Scrabble-loving, cherry-scented wife who takes care of me, too.

I could say she's the full package, and that's all well and good.

But what she truly is . . . is a gift.

THE END

Curious about Max and Henley Rose? Who is the woman who vexes him already? Find out in JOY STICK, where you'll get inside the mind of Max Summers and get to know the woman who drives this ladies' man crazy. For now, here's a sneak peek . . .

I stare across the row of sleek, shiny automobiles, my jaw nearly clanging to the floor.

No way. No fucking way.

The beautiful brunette.

With the long legs.

Killer body.

Smart mouth.

Attitude for miles.

She sports a streak of grease on her cheek and grips a wrench in her hand.

And she grins at me like the cat who has eaten the canary's whole damn family then finished them off with a dish of cream.

She looks at me like she's already won.

But she has no idea who she's up against.

Game on, Henley Rose.

Sign up for my newsletter to receive an alert when these sexy new books are available!

THE ONLY ONE

Here's an excerpt from my novella
THE ONLY ONE, now available!

PROLOGUE

Penny
Ten years ago

The clock mocks me.

As the minute hand ticks closer to eight in the evening, I wrack my brain to figure out if I got the time wrong. Maybe we picked two. Maybe he said ten. Maybe we're meeting tomorrow. My chest twists with a desperate anxiety as I toy with the band on my watch.

But as the fountains of Lincoln Center dance higher under the waning light, I'm sadly certain there was no error in communication.

The only error was one of judgment.

Mine.

Thinking he'd show.

Drawing a deep, frustrated breath, I peer at my watch once more, then raise my face, searching the crowds that wander past the circular aquatic display at Manhattan's epicenter for the performing arts. This fountain is so romantic; that's why we chose it as the place to meet again.

One week later.

Foolishly I hunt for the amber eyes and dark wavy hair, for the lean, tall frame, for that mischievous grin that melts me every time.

I listen for the sound of him amidst the melody of voices, wishing to hear his rise above the others, calling my name, apologizing in that sexy accent of his for being late.

My God, Gabriel's accent was a recipe for making a young woman weak in the knees. That was what he had done to me. The man melted me when I first met him last month in Barcelona at the tail end of my summer of travels across Europe.

When I close my eyes and float back in time, I hear that delicious voice, just a hint of gravel in his tone, and a whole fleet of butterflies chase each other in my belly at the resurgence of that faraway romantic dream.

I open my eyes, trying to blink away the inconvenient intrusion of memory. I should go. It's clear he's not coming tonight.

But, just in case I mixed up the times, maybe I'll give him one more minute. One more look. One more scan of the crowd.

I let the clock tick past eight.

I still don't see him.

I've been here for more than two hours, sitting on the black marble edge of the fountain. Scouring the corners of Lincoln Center. Peering left, then right down Columbus. Circling, like an animal at a zoo—*pathetic modern-day female waiting for male to stay true to his word.*

Sure, one hundred twenty-plus minutes is not much time in the grand scheme of life, but when the person you're waiting for doesn't show, it's a painful eternity of disillusionment.

I wish we had picked midnight to meet because then I'd have an excuse for him. I'd wonder if midnight meant yesterday or perhaps today. But "six in the evening, on the first of the month, as dusk casts its romantic glow over Manhattan"—his words—is perfectly clear.

He was supposed to be on his way to New York for a job. I'd already landed a plum assignment in this city. Fate appeared to have been looking out for us, and so we'd made plans. One week ago, we'd drunk sangria and danced on the sidewalks of Barcelona, to street musicians playing the kind of music that made you want to get close to someone, and he'd cupped my cheek, saying, "I will count down the days, the hours, the minutes until six in the evening on the first day of September."

Then he'd taken me to his room, wearing that dark and dirty look in his hazel eyes. A look that told me how much he wanted me. Words had fallen from his lips over and over that last night in Spain as he'd undressed me, kissed me all over, and sent me soaring. *My Penelope, give me your body. Let me show you pleasure like you've only imagined.*

Cocky bastard.

But he was right. He'd made all my fantasies real.

He'd made love to me with such passion and sensuality that my traitorous body can still remember the imprint of his hands on my skin, the caress of his delicious lips leaving sizzling marks everywhere.

Standing, I run a hand down my pretty red sundress with the tiny white dots and the scoop neck. He loved me in red.

One night we'd walked past a boutique that sold dresses like this. He'd wrapped his arms around me from behind and planted soft, sultry kisses on the back of my neck. "You'd look so lovely in that, my Penelope. And even lovelier when I take it off you. Actually, just wear nothing with me."

I'd shuddered then.

I hurt now as the memory snaps cruelly before my eyes.

I turn away from the fountain, swiping a hand across my cheek. The seed of discouragement planted in the first minutes after he failed to appear has sprouted over the two hours I've waited for him. It's twisted into a thorny weed of disappointment that's lodged deep in my chest.

There are no two ways about it. My three-day love affair under the starry Spanish sky with the man who whispered sweet nothings in my ear while he played my body like a virtuoso pianist isn't getting a second act.

Gabriel has my email.

He knows how to reach me.

He chose not to.

Que sera, sera.

I refuse to cry.

With my chin held high, I walk away.

The rest of the night, the hurt deepens, burrowing into my bones.

The next day, shame wraps itself around that weed in my chest, dominating my emotions. Shame for having believed him. For having bought the damn dress. For having hope.

When I open my closet, I swear the red dress laughs at me. I huff, yank it off the hanger, and stuff it in a grocery bag. I grab the pink one I wore the day I met him, then the soft yellow skirt I had on the next day we were together, which made for such easy access. When I pull down the silky blue tank next, I'm walloped with a reminder of his reaction when he first saw me in it.

His eyes had widened, and he'd groaned appreciatively. "Beautiful."

It was all he'd said, then he'd kissed the hollow of my throat and blazed a sensual trail up my neck, along my jawline to my ear, and whispered, "So beautiful in blue."

I'd melted.

I'd believed all his sweet, swoony words. He'd said so many things that had set my skin on fire, that had made my heart hammer, that had made my panties damp.

Even now, as I clutch the clothes I wore with him, then didn't wear with him, goose bumps rise on my flesh. I squeeze my eyes shut and tell myself to burn the house down.

It's the only way.

I leave my apartment, march ten blocks uptown, and donate the bag of clothes to the nearest Salvation Army.

When I return home, I open my laptop and find the folder with the photos I took of the two of us. I'm tempted, so temped to grab a pint of Ben & Jerry's, run my fingers over the pictures, then download Skype and call his number in Europe to ask why the fuck he didn't show.

But I can't be that girl. I start my first job tomorrow. I need to be a responsible grown-up. I can't be the clingy twenty-one-year-old who isn't able to deal with being ditched.

I'm Penelope Jones, and I can handle anything.

I bring the folder to the trash, then I call up his contact information. His email address. His stupid phone number in Spain. I slide his name to the garbage can, too. My finger hovers over the *empty trash* icon for several interminable seconds that somehow spool into a minute.

But as I remember the way I felt last night, all alone at Lincoln Center, it's wholly necessary to stab the icon.

Let him go.

A clean break.

For the next ten years, I do my best to keep him out of my mind.

Until I see him again.

CHAPTER ONE

Penny
Present day

Shortcake runs free up the steps. She wags her tail the second her white-gloved paws hit the top of the staircase in our building. My sweet little butterscotch Chihuahua-mix glances back from above me, her pink tongue lolling as she pants.

"Show off," I say to her.

Her white-tipped tail vibrates faster and I take that as my cue to bound up the rest of the stairs, my heart still beating hard from our morning run in Central Park. Last summer, when I brought Shortcake home from Little Friends, the animal rescue I run—she'd insisted upon being mine, slathering me in kisses from the second she'd arrived—I never would have imagined she'd also demand to be my running companion. But she's a fast and furious little widget, all seven pounds of her. We're training for a Four-and-Two-Legs-Race that's part of Picnic in the Park to raise money for a coalition of local animal rescues.

When I reach the fourth floor, Shortcake scurries ahead, rushing to the door of the small one-bedroom we share in the upper 90s. It's all ours, and it's near work, so I can't ask for anything more.

With her leash rolled up in one hand, I unlock the door and enter my home. It's my oasis in Manhattan. The walls are painted lavender and yellow, courtesy of a long weekend when my friend Delaney and I went full Martha Stewart and turned the place into a haven of pastels. I'm not normally a pastel girl, but the soothing shades work for me in here. They make me happy.

I like being happy. Crazy, I know.

I fill Shortcake's water dish, and she guzzles nearly all of it down before sprawling on her belly across the cool kitchen floor, arms stretched in front and legs behind, super-dog style.

"By all means, feel free to spend the day lounging," I say to my favorite girl.

She flops to her side.

"I'm totally not jealous of your lifestyle at all," I say as I strip off my exercise clothes then go to take a quick shower.

When I'm done, I grab my phone. I check my daily appointment list as I blow-dry my dark brown hair. Normally, I'm based at the shelter, working with the animals and my volunteers, or heading to the airports to meet the dogs coming in from other states so we can find them homes. Today, though, I need to dress up and put on my best public face. My assistant, Lacey, has set up meetings for me this week with restaurant owners about catering the upcoming picnic. We're in a bit of a bind—the original restaurant slated to cater it had to cancel at the last minute. In a city stuffed with places to feed your face, you might think finding a restaurant is an easy task. But with a date a mere two weeks away, the options narrow quite quickly. So far, my effort to nab an eatery has been a big bust. I've been calling all over town in the last few days, but have yet to come across a restaurant that's both free that day and the right fit.

My quest continues though, since Lacey tracked down four restaurants with openings the day of the picnic. As I twist my hair into a clip, I click on her email.

First up is Dominic Ravini, who runs an Italian joint best known for its "heavenly" spaghetti, Lacey tells me. Bless her. But I just don't think spaghetti is right for a picnic, unless we switch it up to a *Lady and the Tramp* theme.

I peer over at Shortcake. "I'd share a strand of spaghetti with you anytime," I say as I dust on some blush. She thumps her tail against the floor. I take that as a *yes, bring me home pasta for dinner please. With meatballs, of course.*

Next, Lacey writes that I have an appointment with a burrito shop. I give the email a quizzical stare. Though Lacey assures me it's classy, I'm not convinced burritos are the best choice, either. I need to find a restaurant that can strike the perfect balance of sophistication and informality to entice the guests to donate to the shelters but still fit the picnic-in-the-park theme.

That's why I don't hold high hopes for the Indian restaurant she has lined up. Big fan of chana masala here, but I'm not sure it screams *serve me on a paper plate in the park.*

As I reach into my makeup bag, I scroll to the bottom of the email.

The last restaurant with an opening is called *Gabriel's.*

I startle as I read the name and, unexpectedly, my breath catches.

That name.

I freeze, one hand on the mascara wand, the other holding my phone. Even now, years after my valiant attempt to erase that man from my history, his name alone does something to me.

I've dated since him. I've had a few serious boyfriends. But there's still just something about that man. Maybe that's the curse of experiencing the best sex of your life at age twenty-one. At the time, I figured that sex with Gabriel was so great because I didn't know better. Now, I've learned that sleeping with him was mind-blowing because…sleeping with him was mind-blowing.

Those three nights in Spain were magical, passionate, and beyond sensual. I've tried to implement Gabriel amnesia, but he still lingers in the corners of my mind. Letting go of the mascara tube, I take a breath and tell myself a name is just a name. It's a mere coincidence that this eatery on my list shares the same name.

Except…my Gabriel was a cook. A struggling line cook in a small bistro in Barcelona that summer, planning to move to Manhattan for a job here.

I drop my forehead into my hand as a fresh wave of foolishness crashes over me. What if he's been here all these years? What if he came to New York and simply didn't want to see me? What if we've been sharing the same island for the last decade? What if he was married when we were together? What if he went home to his wife, his girlfriend, his lover?

I forced myself to stop playing this *what if* game ten years ago when he didn't show for our rendezvous. I booted him from my brain and refused to linger on him, and especially on all the possible reasons why he left me alone.

Now, he's all I can think about. I need to know if this Gabriel is *my* Gabriel.

When I google the restaurant, I let out an audible groan.

I blink.

Blink again.

Try to still my shaking fingers.

He's here. He's in Manhattan. After a decade, I'm going to come face-to-face with the man who stole my heart and my body.

I set down my phone and scoop up my dog. "Can I send Lacey instead?"

She licks my cheek in reply.

"Is that a yes, Shortcake? As in, you think I should play hooky and spend the day with you and make Lacey do my dirty work?"

This time she administers a longer tongue-lashing.

"Most of the time I'm completely content with the fact that you don't talk," I tell her. "But today is not one of those days."

The mere possibility of seeing him again sets off a storm of warring emotions and confusion inside me. I don't know what to do about this meeting, what to say to him, how I should act. The one thing I'm certain of is that I *need* a two-way conversation, so I call my friend Delaney as I pace around my small living room.

"Hey there," she shouts over the background clatter of construction. "If you can't hear me it's because they're jack-hammering one frigging block away from my spa, which is completely conducive to a restful day of relaxation. Not."

I laugh. "Let me guess. You're walking to work."

"You got it," she says, her normally pretty voice blaring so loudly I have to hold the phone several inches from my ear.

"Speaking of guessing, want to guess who I just found out is on my work schedule today?"

"Tom Hardy? Scott Eastwood? Chris Pine?"

"Henry Cavill," I say, since he's her favorite celebrity. "But seriously, I'm supposed to have a meeting with…" I stop, since I can still hardly believe what I'm about to say. Then I use the nickname we bestowed on Gabriel many moons ago over a bottle of cabernet. "My *international man of mystery.*"

She gasps, and it's loud enough for me to hear her over the racket. "Are you serious?"

I nod. "One hundred percent."

"Okay, hold on," she says, and then ten seconds later, the background noise is sliced away and it's blissfully quiet. "I stepped into the ATM lobby near work. My first massage is in ten minutes, so give me the details."

I dive in and tell her everything I know. "What do I do? Do I go? Do I send Lacey instead? Do I just…*not show?*"

But as I say the last two words, I know I won't do that. I've been on the receiving end of not showing, and I won't stand him up.

"Simple," she says, with authority. "You go."

My stomach drops. Pressing a hand to the wall for balance, I ask, "Are you sure you didn't mean to say I should spend the day working hard at the shelter so that Lacey can have more responsibility overseeing our charitable events?"

Delaney cracks up. "Yes, I'm completely sure I did not say that. Especially since, correct me if I'm wrong, but this is your job, not hers?"

I heave a sigh as I nod. Backing out isn't my style anyway. This is *my* event and *my* responsibility. It's not something I can push off on an assistant who's still learning the ropes. Besides, with one cancellation already, I need to make sure Picnic in the Park comes together. The buck stops with me.

"Yeah, you're right," I say, resigned. "So, um, what do I do? I have no clue how to waltz into his restaurant like he didn't totally devastate me when I stood waiting at Lincoln Center for a man who never showed."

"It's simple," Delaney says in a cool, confident tone.

"How is it simple?"

"Because you're not the same person. You're not that heartbroken twenty-one-year-old about to start a job she did her best to pretend she was going to love because she thought it would please her parents."

"True," I say, some of her confidence rubbing off on me.

I've changed since then. When I went to Spain after college graduation, I was *mostly* sure that I'd be a research analyst on Wall Street. But a small part of me had dreaded that job before it had even started, and that was why I left after only six months. Funny thing—I wasn't the only one to take off from Smith & Holloway. That was the year of exits from the bank, and it became a running joke. First the receptionist, then the human resources manager, then me. "And I love my job now," I say to Delaney, giving myself a pep talk, "and that's why I have to meet with him. Because who cares about him, anyway? The event is more important than his stupid decision to walk away from me."

"Exactly. And you're not the type of woman any sane man should walk away from. So you need to make him eat his heart out."

"I like how you think," I say, a dose of confidence surging through me.

"Leave your hair down, show off that sexy new tattoo, and wear something that makes you look stunning. You look amazing in blue."

I laugh. "He used to say that, too."

"Boom. Done. Get out that royal blue off-the-shoulder top. The sapphire-colored one. Wear it with jeans. Women usually think they need to show their bare legs to be sexy, but a great pair of skinny jeans and heels is hotter than a skirt. Then walk in with your chin held high, like you don't care that he broke your heart."

A grin spreads across my face. "Perfect. That's the opposite of how I dressed when I knew him." I was all about sundresses and cute little skirts when he met me. Young and innocent.

It's time to dress like the woman I am, not the girl I was.

I say good-bye and open my closet. I want to be so god-damn memorable that his jaw drops from the shock, that he falls to his knees and begs forgiveness for standing me up, that he tells me he hasn't gone a day without thinking of me.

Oh yes, I wish for Gabriel to regret with every fiber of his being that he left me alone on what should have been the most romantic reunion of two summer lovers ever.

I slip into my favorite jeans then adjust the shoulder on the top to show off the lily tattoo on my shoulder blade. As I slide my feet into a pair of black flats, I grab my favorite black heels and drop them into my bag. No need to kill myself in four-inch shoes until I arrive at my final meeting.

On the way to my first appointment, I use my phone to take an online crash course in Gabriel Mathias. Since I don't follow the restaurant scene, I had no idea he'd set up shop here. Turns out he's now something of a rising rock-star chef, who recently won a season of a popular reality TV cooking show, then a few months ago he rode that spot of fame to open his first Manhattan establishment. It's the flagship for a bigger business he now runs in cookware, cookbooks, and more.

Well, la-de-dah. The once-struggling cook who excelled at paella has gone from rags to riches.

I grit my teeth when I see the first photo of him. He's still gorgeous. Actually, I should revise that. He's even more gorgeous.

The fucker.

But I'm not going to let his looks soften me. I'm not going to be swayed by his pretty face. I'm strong, and I'm tough, and I'm smart, too. Which means I need to be prepared.

I find a clip from his show on YouTube as I walk along Eighth Avenue. Popping in my headphones, I hit play and brace myself.

Do not let that sexy accent woo you. Do not stare at those kissable lips.

I do my best to listen objectively, as if he's a test subject in a lab. A host or producer off-camera asks him a question. "You lost tonight's appetizer battle. What do you think that does for your chances to win it all?"

"It makes it tougher for me to win," he says in that warm, sexy voice I adored. "But I'm ready for the challenge. I'll need to work harder on the main course match."

I scoff as I march down the sidewalk. What will these reality geniuses come up with next? Salad showdown? Dessert skirmish?

"How did you feel losing to Angelique when you've been making a name for yourself as a master of appetizers?"

Gabriel takes a breath, his chest rising and falling. Then the corner of his lips curves up. "I was frustrated with myself but not so angry that I'd have, say, thrown a phone."

A laugh comes from off-camera, and I can only imagine the producers huddled together to try to incite him to throw a phone over a fallen flan, or a run-of-the-mill risotto.

The screen flashes, and the video clip cuts to what looks to be the end of the episode with the host holding Gabriel's hand high in the air. I guess he won the match in the end, and his phone was safe from damage.

As I stop at the crosswalk, I return to my original search. My eyes widen when I dig deeper and find stories of his official win on the cooking show, and all the names the media bestowed on him.

The sexiest chef.

The hottest cook.

The heartbreaker in the kitchen.

Nearly every article comes with a photo of him. I click on the first few. Then another set. Then one more group of pics. My chest burns with annoyance. My muscles tighten with anger.

In every single picture of the chef du jour, he has a different woman on his arm.

That's my answer as to why he never showed. Gabriel is a ladies' man. A bad boy. The consummate playboy, out with a new beautiful babe every single night.

As I head in to my meeting with the Italian chef, I hope against hope this man can do something amazing with spaghetti at a picnic so I can call off the rest of my appointments.

He can't.

Then, it turns out the burrito man is now booked for another event.

At the Indian restaurant, the manager tells me it would be his first time catering an event, and he can only cook for fifty.

We're expecting more than three hundred. I thank him with a smile, then sigh heavily as I leave and head to the Village to see the man who swept me off my feet once upon a time.

As the train chugs into the station, I change my shoes then tug on my top, showing a bit more shoulder than I usually do. He *loved* to kiss me there. He loved tattoos, too. I didn't have any then. I have three now, including the lily. Let him look. Let him stare.

I slick on lip gloss as I leave the subway, check my reflection in the shop window on the corner, and make my way to Gabriel's on Christopher Street. My heart beats double time.

When I reach the brick-front eatery on the corner of two cobbled streets, I'm more impressed than I want to be. His restaurant is so cool and hip and sexy, with a dash of old-fashioned charm in the hanging wooden sign.

I narrow my eyes and nearly breathe a plume of fire onto the entryway. He probably charms the female patrons with his witty words, his panty-melting grin, and his fucking amazing food.

Then takes them to his bed and runs his tongue…

Stop. Just stop.

I clench my fists then take a breath, letting it spread through my body. I remind myself I'm here for business. I'm here for the dogs. This is my chance to raise a lot of money for a cause that matters dearly to me.

When the hostess greets me and I tell her I have a meeting with Gabriel, a part of me hopes that he's grown a paunch, acquired a receding hairline, or perhaps lost a tooth in a barroom brawl.

But as he strides toward where I wait by the door, the saying *take my breath away* means something entirely new.

Oxygen flees my body.

The twenty-four-year-old guy who dazzled me when I gave him my virginity a decade ago has nothing on this man in front of me.

He's as beautiful as heartbreak. With cheekbones carved by the masters, eyes the color of topaz, and hair that's now shoulder-length, he's somehow impossibly sexier. My fingers itch to touch those dark strands. My skin sizzles as images of him moving over me flicker fast before my eyes.

I try to focus on the here and now, but the here and now makes my heart hammer with desire. Everything about him exudes confidence, charm, and sex appeal, even his casual clothes. He wears black jeans, lace-up boots, and a well-worn V-neck T-shirt that reveals his lean, toned, inked arms. He had several when I knew him—now his arms are nearly covered in artwork, and they're stunning. His ink is so incredibly seductive.

He holds out a hand and flashes me that grin that makes me want to grab the neck of his shirt, yank him close, and say *kiss me now like you did all those nights before.*

Instead, he takes my palm in his then presses his lips to the top of my hand, making my head spin. Then he speaks, his accent like an opiate. He's French and Brazilian, and I don't know which side dominates his voice. I don't care, either, because the mixture of the two is delicious. "I've been looking forward to seeing you, Penny."

Oh God. Oh shit. He's excited to see me.

My stupid heart dances.

I swallow, trying to tap in to the section of my brain that's capable of language. I part my lips, but my mouth imitates the Sahara. I dig down deep, somehow finding the power of speech, and manage a parched, "Hello."

So much for playing it cool.

"Shall we sit down?" he asks, his delicious voice as sensual as it was that summer.

Yes, and tell me you're sorry. Tell me you were trapped in a cave, that spies stole your phone, that you were offered the job of the century in Nepal and you couldn't bear to see me again because then you'd never have taken the gig. You had no choice, clearly. Seeing me would have made it impossible to resist me.

Because that would be him eating his goddamn heart out.

Instead, I'm greeted with another enchanting smile as he says, "It's so good to meet you. I want to hear all about your charity and to see if we can work together for your event. My business manager believes this could be a great partnership for us both." He gestures to a quiet booth in the far corner. The lunchtime rush hasn't begun. I sit, then he slides across from me.

As I begin to share information with him about Little Friends, a fresh, cold wave of understanding washes over me.

He doesn't recognize me, and I honestly don't look that different than I did ten years ago.

Which means…he doesn't remember me.

ACKNOWLEDGEMENTS

Thank you to Helen Williams for the gorgeous cover! Thank you to KP Simmon for all the things. Big hugs to Kelley for running the ship, and to Candi and Keyanna for all they do. Huge gratitude to my girls, Laurelin, CD and Kristy, and a special shoutout to Lili Valente.

Big love Jen McCoy and Dena Marie, who loved Chase and Josie, and helped bring their magic to the page. I am grateful to Lauren McKellar for her keen eye, to Karen Lawson for her eagle eye, to Janice for her fine attention to detail.

Thank you to my family and my husband, and to my fabulous dogs! Most of all thanks to YOU – the reader.

Xoxo
Lauren

Also by Lauren Blakely

BIG ROCK, the hit New York Times
Bestselling standalone romantic comedy!

MISTER O, also a New York Times
Bestselling standalone romantic comedy!

WELL HUNG, a New York Times
Bestselling standalone romantic comedy!

THE SEXY ONE, a swoony New York Times
Bestselling standalone romance!

The New York Times and USA Today Bestselling
Seductive Nights series including *Night After Night*,
After This Night, and *One More Night*

And the two standalone romance novels,
Nights With Him and *Forbidden Nights*, both
New York Times and USA Today Bestsellers!

Sweet Sinful Nights, *Sinful Desire*, *Sinful Longing*
and *Sinful Love*, the complete New York Times
Bestselling high-heat romantic suspense series that
spins off from Seductive Nights!

Playing With Her Heart, a USA Today
bestseller, and a sexy Seductive Nights spin-off
standalone! (Davis and Jill's romance)

21 Stolen Kisses, the USA Today
Bestselling forbidden new adult romance!

Caught Up In Us, a New York Times and
USA Today Bestseller! (Kat and Bryan's romance!)

Pretending He's Mine, a Barnes & Noble and
iBooks Bestseller! (Reeve & Sutton's romance)

Trophy Husband, a New York Times and
USA Today Bestseller! (Chris & McKenna's romance)

Far Too Tempting, the USA Today Bestselling
standalone romance! (Matthew and Jane's romance)

Stars in Their Eyes, an iBooks bestseller!
(William and Jess' romance)

My USA Today bestselling
No Regrets series that includes

The Thrill of It
(Meet Harley and Trey)

and its sequel

Every Second With You

My New York Times and USA Today
Bestselling Fighting Fire series that includes

Burn For Me
(Smith and Jamie's romance!)

Melt for Him
(Megan and Becker's romance!)

and *Consumed by You*
(Travis and Cara's romance!)

The Sapphire Affair series...
The Sapphire Affair
The Sapphire Heist

CONTACT

I love hearing from readers! You can find me on Twitter at LaurenBlakely3, or Facebook at LaurenBlakelyBooks, or online at LaurenBlakely.com. You can also email me at laurenblakelybooks@gmail.com

CPSIA information can be obtained
at www.ICGtesting.com
Printed in the USA
LVOW01s2318250417
532183LV00008B/396/P